U.S. MARSHAL JUBAL STONE TERRITORY

FORBIDDEN LOVE ON THE TEXAS FRONTIER

CASEY NASH

JANA JAMES

Copyright © 2021 by Casey Nash and Jana James

Published by Magnolia Blossom Publishing

All rights reserved. No part of this publication may be reproduced, distributed, or transmitted in any form or by any means, including photocopying, recording, or other electronic or mechanical methods, without the prior written permission of the publisher, except in the case of brief quotations embodied in critical reviews and certain other noncommercial uses permitted by copyright law.

ISBN: 9798451372364

❀ Created with Vellum

CHAPTER 1

The train stopped in Hearne long enough for Marshal Jubal Stone and his deputy, Tanner Burns, to grab a sandwich at one of the diners and a cup of coffee. Then the whistle blew, and the lawmen climbed back aboard for their final destination: Palestine.

When the train pulled into the depot, Jubal stared out the small glass window. Memories of this small town began flooding his mind. He remembered when he first met Monty Peel as a sixteen-year-old and shortly afterward signed on as his deputy. Peel taught Jubal not only how to be a lawman but how to be a decent human being. There was a kindness about Monty that everyone liked.

"Marshal, Marshal," said Tanner, trying to get Jubal's attention as the train stopped.

"Yeah, Tanner." Stone stood immediately to his feet, almost embarrassed at the delayed response to his deputy. Then, he pulled on his hat and moved quickly out into the aisle toward the door. As Jubal stepped off the train, he immediately felt a soberness in the air. People were walking up and down the boardwalks with their heads down. It was eerie, something he'd never seen before in his previous years serving there as deputy. The town of Palestine was in mourning, deep mourning. Their beloved sheriff, Monty Joseph Peel, was about to be laid to rest.

"Tanner, fetch the horses and meet me down at the church. It's at the end of town, yonder way." Jubal pointed.

"All right, Jubal. Say," Tanner held out his hand, "why the church? Figured it would be at Mr. Peel's house."

Stone chuckled as he reached for his watch just inside his vest. It read 2:31. It was now less than thirty minutes until Monty's service. Jubal snapped the cover over it and put it back in his pocket as he looked over at Tanner. "His house wasn't much. I figure the town council needed more room for those who'll attend."

Stone walked slowly down the boardwalk until he heard a man say his name, softly. "Hello, Marshal Stone." It was Ted Harris, the town barber. Tears ran down his face. "I know Monty would have appreciated you coming."

Jubal touched his hat. "Good to see you, Mr. Harris." They shook hands.

"I can't believe he's gone, Jubal. And what those devils did to him, well... it still makes me sick to my stomach."

"I don't know what you mean, Mr. Harris. I only heard that Roberts and his gang killed Monty and shot up his deputy."

"They killed him, all right. They tied him to the back of a wagon and dragged his body down Main Street. I saw it from the stoop of my shop. Sheriff Peel told us an hour before they arrived not to brace them. He feared that those who took up arms against Roberts and his mongrels would be killed."

Jubal stood speechless. His whole body was aquiver. He felt the strength go out of his legs. This was the first he'd heard of how his dear friend Monty Peel had been murdered and he wasn't taking it well, not at all.

"Well, I best get on down to the church. Sheriff Peel's services will be starting shortly," said Harris. Ted ran a comb over his head to groom the few hairs that were blowing in the wind. Then, with his hand, he brushed down his clothes as he questioned Jubal. "Have you seen Rosy yet?"

Stone didn't answer, still stunned from Harris' painful description of Monty's death. "Marshal Stone... Marshal Stone." Ted put his hand to Jubal's shoulder with a look of worry.

Finally, Jubal shook his head and responded, "Pardon me. What did you say, Mr. Harris?"

"I asked if you've seen Rosy since you arrived in town? You know she and the sheriff were to be married the day after he retired, which would have been tomorrow. We had a man coming to Palestine to take his place. You know Monty." Harris's face wrinkled. "He wasn't going to retire until the new man was installed."

Jubal's mind once again ran wild, recollecting the first time he ever met Rosy at the diner. *Boy, she and Monty lit into each other. They acted as if they couldn't tolerate the sight of one another. But... everybody in town knew that was all a show. I saw them wink at each other more than once. And Rosy, why, she lit up every time she saw Monty come through the door. Reckon there wasn't a day he didn't put his boots under one of her tables in her diner.*

"Bring that back here, you blame dog," came an angry voice from up the street. Jubal looked down to see a hound running his way. It was Lep, Monty's brindle-colored cur, and he had something in his mouth.

"Hey, Lep, ol' boy," said Jubal as he knelt and petted the hound exuberantly on the head. "What you got there?" He wrangled the hat from his jaws. It was Monty's Stetson. Tears streamed down Jubal's face as he stood up and dusted the dirt from the brim. In that moment, Jubal's mind went back in time. *Monty loved this hat. From the second his feet hit the floor, he pulled it on,* he chuckled to himself. *Black hat and white, long handles. Monty, you were a sight to behold and not a pretty one.* He stared up into the sky and shook his head. *I remember that peckerwood that made the mistake of knocking this off the chair you were sitting in over at the Thirsty Hog Saloon. You wiped the floor up with 'im. His partner, I recollect, packed a pretty good punch.* Jubal touched his jaw. *But I reckon I got the best of that Jasper.*

Jubal stared down at Lep. His big brown eyes stared back. He whimpered and licked his chops as if waiting for his evening meal.

Jubal reached down and gently stroked his head, remembering how he hardly ever saw Monty without his four-legged friend at heel.

"That dang mongrel," said an angry, out of breath, Elbert Dawson, Waco's undertaker. He was joined by two others, his assistant, Horace Wheatly, and a young, scrawny-looking kid. All three of them stood there, panting like they had been in a race down Main Street.

"Well, Marshal Stone," said Elbert, gasping for air as he extended his hand.

Jubal reciprocated. "Mr. Dawson. I figure you're looking for this." He handed Elbert the hat. Lep stared up, following it with his eyes then jumping up on the undertaker's legs. Dawson slapped the cur on the muzzle and irritably dusted off his black suit. As he looked up to Jubal, he saw the marshal's displeasure and stopped what he was doing.

Smiling sheepishly, he confessed, "I just had these duds cleaned." He slowly reached down to pet the dog until he saw flashing teeth and heard a deep growl.

"Easy, Lep," said Stone as he gently pulled him by the scruff of the neck. "Mr. Dawson, I believe you have what you came for. We'll see you directly at the church, me and... Lep, unless you object." The marshal crossed his arms and waited for Dawson's response.

Elbert tugged at his shirt collar as if it were choking him, then he looked down at Lep and back to Jubal. "Why, no, of course not." Then, he stared sternly at his assistants. "Well, you heard the man. Rattle your hocks and let's get this hat back on the table beside Sheriff Peel where it belongs." He offered up a slight, but nervous, wave and trotted off back toward the church.

Jubal pulled his belt from around his jeans and tethered it to Lep's collar. "Let's go, boy. Monty's waiting."

Stone and the cur walked down the middle of Main Street. A few people on the boardwalks stared and a couple pointed. "That's Marshal Jubal Stone with Sheriff Peel's hound. Looks like they're headed for the church," someone said.

As Jubal got closer to the small, wood-framed church, there was a large crowd of people collected just outside the door, chattering.

When they saw Stone and Lep, they suddenly got quiet and stepped aside, giving the two clear passage. When through the door, Jubal looked up the aisle to the open coffin. Standing beside it, greeting those expressing their condolences, was Rosy.

I ain't looking forward to this, he thought to himself. *Lord, give me the strength to be strong, for Rosy's sake and the folks of Palestine.*

Jubal and Lep took their place in line and waited to reach the front. When Rosy made eye contact with Stone, she began to weep loudly and held her arms out to him. He stepped forward and embraced her. Whispering in her ear, he said, "I'm sorry, Rosy. Monty was the best. Hope you don't mind me bringing a friend." Jubal slowly pushed her away and they both looked down.

"Lep. You little bandit, stealing Monty's hat." Rosy knelt down and stroked the hound's head. "You miss him too, don't you, boy?" She looked up to Jubal. "Monty and Lep were inseparable. You never saw one without the other. He's whined and whimpered ever since Monty was…" Rosy put her hand to her mouth. "Killed."

"Yep, Monty sure took a shine to him. I remember the day you give him Lep, Rosy."

AFTER THE FUNERAL service in the church, Rosy, Jubal, and Lep walked before the horse-drawn carriage until it reached Peach Orchard Cemetery. There, the preacher said a few words over Monty before four men lowered his pine box into the ground with two ropes.

Spontaneously, Jubal pulled out his flute and tapped it against his leg. Then, he stepped forward, put it to his lips, and played a mighty fine-sounding ditty. When finished, he looked down at his friend's coffin and nodded. "That was your favorite, Monty. But it don't hold a candle to the golden harps you're hearing about now. Say hello to my folks for me."

Rosy stepped forward and squeezed his arm. "That was beautiful, Jubal." Then she knelt down, picked up a handful of dirt, and tossed it on top of the big pine box. Jubal did the same.

Then, the marshal slowly drew his pistol and pulled out his knife. Carving a notch in the handle, he looked up at the sky and said, "This is for you, Monty. I'll never forget you, pard." Stone's bottom lip quivered as he notched his pistol. Some gunmen cut a sliver out of their wooden handles to record their killings, a vain symbol of their pride. Jubal's pistol notches, however, represented the names of several lawmen who had died while carrying out their duties. It was his way of honoring them.

Shoving the Colt back into the holster, Stone reached and took Rosy's hand in his. The parson slowly closed his Bible and ended the service with prayer. At the amen, the two grave diggers grabbed the handles of their shovels sticking out of the pile of dirt a few feet away and began filling in the hole from which it came.

Jubal put his arm around Rosy to escort her back to town. After taking a few steps, she turned to see if Lep was following. He wasn't. The hound was at the edge of Monty's grave, sniffing, whining, and digging in the loose dirt, protesting the men covering up his master. Rosy shook her head and began to wail. "Poor fellow. He'll be lost without Monty."

Stone clicked to Lep and patted his pant leg, trying to get him to follow, but the brindle hound didn't come. In fact, he lay down next to Monty's grave and rested his head on his front paws. Jubal wiped the tears from his eyes then looked around to Rosy. "I'll come back and fetch him later, Rosy."

Tanner looked on at Lep and felt sorry for the dog as did many standing around Monty's grave.

As Rosy and Stone reached the edge of town, they stepped up on the boardwalk. Walking slowly along, Rosy squeezed Jubal's arm and through tears said, "Did you hear that Monty and I were planning to get hitched?"

Stone smiled warmly. "I sure did, Rosy. That ol' mossback, Monty. What took him so long, you reckon?"

Rosy chuckled then stopped and put her hands to her hips. "That's what I asked him. You know what he said?" She continued before Jubal could answer. "He didn't want me to become a widow. Said being sheriff was a dangerous job and as long as he wore the badge he didn't want to marry."

Jubal nodded, but then his mind raced back to Waco where his new bride was. A shiver went down his spine. *I hope Nancy never has to drink from that well. Monty's right, toting a gun and wearing a badge is...*

Suddenly, Stone's thoughts were interrupted by Rosy's question. "By the way, Jubal, how's that young bride of yours doing? Monty and I were looking forward to attending the wedding until Roberts and his gang changed our plans."

"Nancy's just fine." He patted Rosy's arm. "I hope the two of you can meet soon."

"Me too, Jubal. Me too. I can tell by that smile on your face that she's a real peach."

"Yes, ma'am, she is. I'm lucky to have found her."

"She's lucky to have you, Jubal. I know you'll make a wonderful husband to her."

Suddenly, Rosy stopped on the boardwalk and turned to the young marshal. The expression on her face told Stone that what she was about to say was serious. "Jubal, I reckon to tell you not to go after Monty's killers would be like trying to stop the Texas wind from blowing, but please think of that new wife of yours. What if something happens to you? She would be a widow."

Jubal rubbed the back of his neck nervously and stared down at the wooden planks under his feet. On the one hand, he agreed with Rosy's assessment that going after Judd Roberts could cost him his life and make Nancy a young widow, but on the other hand, bringing killers to justice was part and parcel of being a marshal. To boot, Roberts and his boys killed one of the best men, in Jubal's estimation, whoever wore skin.

Jubal cleared his throat. "Monty would have done the same for me. He gave me a chance, Rosy, to be more than a man traveling the rails. Made me his deputy, you remember?"

"I remember, Jubal." Rosy dug around in the small bag she was carrying and pulled out something very shiny and cupped it to her chest. Then, slowly opening her hand, she said, "I want you to have this, Jubal, to remember Monty by." It was Peel's badge.

Jubal raised his hands in protest. "No, Rosy. That's something you should keep. And as for needing something to remember Monty by, I've got a mind full of memories." He tapped his finger against his temple.

Rosy pushed the badge toward Jubal again. "You were like a son to Monty, Jubal, dear. Please… take it. Monty would like that."

Stone's eyes filled with tears as he gently opened his hand and took the badge. Then, he smiled. "I recollect the first time I woke up and saw this pinned to the big man's shirt." Jubal held up the tin star. "It was right over yonder, under that lean-to."

"I remember that morning, Jubal. Monty brought you into the diner and told me to keep feeding you until you were full."

"All the biscuits, bacon, and eggs I could eat." Jubal smiled at Rosy, then he snapped his fingers. "You two had me fooled for over a week or more, the way you went back and forth at each other. That first day, I figured you didn't much like Monty, but it didn't take me long to catch you two lovebirds a-winking and a-smiling."

"Well, Jubal, if you want to know the truth," Rosy bumped his elbow and grinned. "When I first came to Palestine and opened the diner, I wasn't too impressed with Monty Peel. His manners were more like a billy goat than a man. And loud—I declare—with that big, booming voice he'd bark, 'Rosy, another cup of coffee. Just bring the pot.'"

Jubal shook his head. "By jingo, he sure did like his coffee strong and hot. And for the manners, I figure you rubbed the rough spots off of him pretty good."

Rosy chuckled. "I tried. I tried. What I wouldn't give to serve him up another cup of coffee and hear his voice. I never met a man kinder than Monty Peel. That's what made me fall in love with him."

Jubal and Rosy reached her diner and walked inside. Rosy removed her black hat and hung it on the rack. Jubal pulled off his Stetson and did the same. Jacob Wheeler, one of her new employees, came in behind them.

"Sit down, Miss Rosy, you and the marshal, and I'll fetch you both a cup of coffee. Won't take me but three shakes of a lamb's tail."

"All right, Jacob. That sounds good." She looked back to Stone as he pulled out a chair for her. "Jubal, do you have time for a cup of coffee?"

"Sure do, Rosy." He sat down beside her and looked back toward the kitchen. "Who's that pleasant young fellow working the kitchen?"

"That's Jacob Wheeler. You know who talked me into hiring him?"

"His ma?" chuckled Jubal.

"No, silly." Rosy tapped Stone's hand on the table as a slight rebuke. "Monty."

"Sure enough?" Jubal asked.

"Yup. Monty brought Jacob into the diner about three months back, sat him down over there at that table, and told me to fill him up with biscuits, bacon, eggs, and coffee. Sound familiar, Jubal?"

Stone nodded and smiled as he leaned back in his chair.

With his back, Jacob pushed through the double doors leading out of the kitchen carrying two cups of hot coffee on a tray. He walked to Rosy and the marshal's table and placed them down in front of them.

Jubal pulled out a chair and looked up at Wheeler. "Sit yourself down, Jacob. Rosy tells me that Sheriff Peel was the one that got you in the traces here."

Jacob Wheeler had come into Palestine on the rails, busted up, broke, and hungry. Sheriff Peel bandaged his knife wound, filled his gizzard with food from Rosy's Diner, and helped secure a job for him so he could take care of himself. This was a few months before the sheriff's untimely death, dragged behind a wagon by Judd Roberts and his gang.

Jacob Wheeler decided to stay a week in Palestine, then another. Now, three months later, the small Texas town had become his home.

Rosy, Sheriff Peel's wife-to-be, took a shine to the young, lanky Northerner from Boston, Massachusetts and put him to work. The sandy-blond haired fellow had impeccable manners and a relentless resolve to better himself. Rosy had recently discovered that he possessed quite the culinary skills in the kitchen.

Recently, Jacob confided in Rosy that someday he would like to own his own restaurant, an upscale version of her diner, that would have on its menu some of the dishes served up in the East. Jacob's only problem was that he was extremely shy, the quiet type who would rather work behind closed doors than meet the public.

However, Elizabeth Dubois, Mayor Edward Dubois' daughter, who had become a frequent diner at Rosy's restaurant, had noticed Jacob and aimed to get him to notice her, even if it meant she had to risk appearing forward to do so.

"Yes, sir. He sure did recommend me," answered Jacob, "and I'm mighty obliged to him and Miss Rosy for taking a chance on me."

"How did you take to riding the rails?"

Jacob shifted around in his chair. "I didn't cotton to it at all, Marshal." He raised his shirt and showed Jubal his scar. "Near got fileted by two men who wanted my plunder."

"Did they get it?"

"Yeah, they did, but I give 'em more than they asked for."

Jubal smiled. He liked Jacob's grit. "How's that?"

"I wrestled the knife from the one doing the cutting. Then, he and his partner bolted for the door. They threw my bag of belongings out and both jumped. Sheriff Peel bandaged my wound and brought me in here for some vittles. That's when I met Miss Rosy."

"Jacob is a good worker and a mighty fine cook. We sure do miss Monty, don't we, Jacob?" said Rosy.

The young man's eyes watered and his lips puckered. He tried to speak but he couldn't. Then, he cleared his throat and with his sleeve wiped his tears. "Marshal Stone, Sheriff Peel talked a lot about you. Told me that you, like myself, came in on the train one day and stayed. He also said you were the best deputy he'd ever had and how proud he was that you became a sheriff and then a marshal."

Now, Jubal was the one having trouble holding back his emotions. Jacob's words about Monty caused him to look away and fight back tears. He was the closest person to a father Jubal had since his own pa had been killed.

Rosy reached across the table and patted Jubal's hand. "Well, aren't we a pitiful sight, the three of us. Reckon what Monty would say if he saw us sitting around, eulogizing him?"

Jubal sat up and took hold of his cup of coffee. Taking a big, long gulp, he set the mug down on the table and smiled. "He'd say, 'What the Sam Hill is going on around here?'" Jubal threw his voice, sounding just like Monty.

Rosy slapped the table and hollered with laughter, as did Jacob. "If I didn't know better, Jubal, I'd swear Monty was here in the diner saying them very words," she said, wiping away tears of laughter.

The three of them continued to share their stories about Monty over coffee and some apple pie that Rosy had baked early that morning. Customers were beginning to come into the diner for supper. Jacob reached for the apron he had laid over a chair before he sat down and tied it on. "Ms. Baker, I'll take care of the customers if you and the marshal want to keep visiting."

Stone pushed back on the chair and rose. "Figure I'll take a walk around town, maybe go by and meet the sheriff. He spoke to me at the funeral and asked me to come by afterward. Woodrow Wright, I believe was his name."

Rosy stood and pulled Jubal to her. She leaned over and gave him a kiss on the cheek. "Thank you for coming. I sure hope I can find someone to take Lep. I can't bear to see him grieve so."

"I wouldn't have missed coming, Rosy," Jubal said as he patted her on the hand. Then, he said, "I'll find Lep a home, even if I have to take him myself." He pulled out Peel's badge. "And thanks for this. I'll cherish it for the rest of my life." Turning to Wheeler, he held out his hand. "Jacob, it was a pleasure to meet you, sir. Take care of Rosy."

"I certainly will, Marshal," replied Jacob as he continued to hold firmly Jubal's hand. "I would like to speak with you before you leave town."

"How about breakfast in the morning? Know of a good place to eat?"

They both laughed, as did Rosy. She walked toward the customers coming in. That's when Jacob leaned in and said, "I want to tell you what I know about Monty's death and the men that caused it. I'll see you in the morning."

Wheeler's words piqued Stone's interest. "I'll see you around six, Jacob. I need to catch up with my deputy. He might get lost in the big town of Palestine." Jubal smiled.

"Sounds good, Marshal. I'll cook us up some flapjacks and bacon and have a pot of coffee on the boil."

CHAPTER 2

A cloud scuttled past the bright afternoon sun as Elizabeth Dubois stood stoically at her father's side, listening to the preacher's words before Sheriff Peel's coffin was lowered into the ground. Her heart broke for Rosy as she watched her new friend speak to the marshal who had played a farewell tune on his flute for the sheriff.

Elizabeth wanted to hurry to Rosy's side and hug her, but she knew if she moved from her spot next to her father, a lecture on the proper conduct of a young lady of position would follow as soon as they stepped into their carriage. Elizabeth's mother stood on her father's right, and Elizabeth knew her mother would frown if she made any attempt to show overt consideration for what her mother considered the simple people of the town. Elizabeth prayed for Rosy and the town of Palestine as they walked forward in life without their beloved sheriff.

Twenty-two-year-old Elizabeth had returned to Palestine from teacher's college three weeks before Sheriff Peel's death, and since there was no opening at the local school, she was still living at home under her father's domineering thumb.

When Rosy turned to leave the cemetery, Mayor Dubois took his wife's elbow and guided her toward their carriage. Elizabeth followed dutifully. She caught Rosy's eye and hoped she portrayed in her look what she felt in her heart. She'd go to the diner later and offer Rosy any support she needed.

Once settled in the carriage, Elizabeth brushed a few wrinkles from her black mourning dress skirt. Oh, how she disliked wearing black. Not only did it deepen her sadness, seeing herself dressed in black from head to toe, but her normally lustrous, dark brown hair dulled under the black hat. Perhaps it was the tight bun at the nape of her neck instead of her usual loose curls that added to her somber mood, but it was proper, and if there was one thing people said about Elizabeth it was that she was proper.

She slowly shook her head as her father guided the carriage away from the cemetery, wishing her father didn't insist that the family follow each of his ridiculous rules. This was Palestine, not New York, but the mayor had let his position go to his head, and everyone near him paid the price.

Being the only child of Edward and Dorothea Dubois was trying. More than once, her mother had told Elizabeth that her father would have preferred a son. Regardless of her father's wishes, she was not his son and never could be. He would have to accept her for who she was and allow her to live her life.

The mayor dropped off his wife and daughter at their grand home before heading back to his office. Before Elizabeth and Dorothea set foot on the porch, their smiling housekeeper opened the front door, greeting them both, and took their shawls.

Elizabeth said, "Mother, I'm going to go upstairs and change, and then I'm going to go for a walk. The funeral this afternoon was heartbreaking, and I need some time to think."

Dorothea stared at her daughter and asked, "Why should today upset you? A sheriff should expect that he could be killed at any moment, and the rest of the town should have anticipated that. I don't understand why everyone walks around with glum faces."

Elizabeth knew her mother would never understand so she simply replied, "The people in the town loved Sheriff Peel. Of course, they're going to be upset. I just want to walk out in the fresh air and enjoy life. If Mrs. Crandall does retire at the end of the school term, I would like to apply for the position. The more people I meet, the easier it will be for me to convince everyone that I would make a good teacher."

Dorothea shook her head again. "You don't understand how these things work, my dear. Your father is the mayor. If he decides you should be the new teacher, the council will go along with him. However, I would not count on that. Your father wants you to marry well, and he has his eye out for a proper gentleman to come courting and ask for your hand."

Elizabeth turned her head so her mother could not see her eyes roll before answering, "I plan to marry for love, Mother, not for any gain financial or otherwise. Please try to explain to Father that I don't want to meet the man he thinks would suit me. I will find my own husband in time. In the meantime, I would like to teach. I didn't go off to college and get my teaching certificate so I could sit at home and entertain the men that Father thinks will help him in business or with his political aspirations."

Dorothea shooed off her daughter with her hands and said, "Go for your walk. You definitely need to clear your head, and I need a cup of tea. Don't be late for supper."

Elizabeth retreated to her room and removed the ugly black dress as quickly as she could. She said a small prayer that she would not have to wear it again anytime soon. She loosened the bun from her neck and gave her head a shake, freeing her black curls. Dressing quickly in a navy skirt and a light blue blouse that accentuated her blue eyes, Elizabeth tied back her curls with a bright blue ribbon and hurried downstairs.

After pinning her small hat to her head, she slipped out of the front door quietly before her mother could offer any more advice. She was heading for the diner to offer Rosy support and see the handsome man who caught her eye the first time she had entered the diner. Jacob Wheeler was the type of man who interested Elizabeth, but if her father knew, he would be horrified because Jacob was everything her father didn't like.

Strolling toward the diner, Elizabeth greeted everyone she saw. As each person returned her smile or said hello, Elizabeth's hopes grew that the town council might choose her to teach the children of Palestine.

Reaching the diner, Elizabeth peered into the front window but didn't see Rosy. Her heart sped up when she did see Jacob. There was something about the man that intrigued her.

Putting on her best smile, Elizabeth entered the diner and took an empty table near the front. Jacob hurried over and asked if she wanted coffee or tea.

"I'd like a cup of tea and a slice of pie if you have some," Elizabeth answered.

"Rosy baked apple pies this morning. I'll get you a slice," Jacob said before hurrying off toward the kitchen.

Elizabeth watched Jacob disappear into the kitchen and wondered how she could get him to speak to her or treat her differently than he did every other diner customer. When Jacob returned, he set the slice of pie and teacup on the table.

"Will there be anything else, ma'am?" he asked.

"You know," Elizabeth said. "I've been coming in here for three weeks, and everyone calls you Jacob. I think you could call me by name. My name is Elizabeth Dubois, but my friends call me Beth."

"Umm, yes, ma'am, I mean Miss Dubois. I could do that," Jacob stammered.

Elizabeth smiled. "I didn't mean for you to call me Miss Dubois. Please, call me Beth or Elizabeth if you insist. My father thinks it more appropriate, but I like Beth. My friends at the teacher's college all called me Beth."

Jacob stood there looking as if lightning had struck him. He swallowed noticeably and nodded before he said, "I will try and remember that, Miss Beth."

"I hope you do. I've only been in Palestine for three weeks, as I said. When I left for teacher's college, we lived in New Orleans. I like this small town better, and I could use friends. We could be friends, don't you think?" Elizabeth asked as she lifted the teacup for a sip.

"Umm, sure, Miss Beth, we could be friends," Jacob managed to say. "Do you need anything else?"

"Is Rosy here?" Elizabeth asked. "I didn't have a chance to talk to her at the funeral earlier."

"She stepped out but will be back shortly. I'll tell her you'd like to speak to her," Jacob answered before turning on his heels and walking quickly to the kitchen before Elizabeth had a chance to say anything else.

Elizabeth was finishing her pie when Rosy walked up to her table. "Hi, Beth, it's so good to see you."

Elizabeth stood and hugged Rosy tightly. "I'm so sorry I couldn't speak to you or offer condolences at Sheriff Peel's funeral. You know how my father is. He didn't think we should mingle with what he refers to as the 'common people.'"

Rosy laughed. "He needs to change his attitude. When election time rolls around, it will be us common people who will decide whether or not he remains mayor."

"That's quite true," Elizabeth said. "Please sit awhile and tell me how you're doing."

Rosy sat down next to Elizabeth and said, "I'm doing as well as can be expected."

"I wish I had some words to make this easier." Elizabeth reached for her hand.

"Knowing you and the residents of Palestine care means a lot, and I'll get through this," Rosy promised.

Jacob approached the table and asked Rosy if she needed anything. When she said she didn't, Jacob turned to Elizabeth and swallowed.

"Can I get you anything else, Miss Beth?" Jacob asked.

Elizabeth answered with a broad smile. "No, thank you, Jacob."

As soon as Jacob was back in the kitchen, Rosy leaned closer to Elizabeth and said, "He called you Miss Beth. How did you manage that?"

Elizabeth shrugged. "I asked him to after I introduced myself, and I think I rambled on about Father insisting I use the name Elizabeth. Maybe he felt sorry for me."

"He's a nice young man," Rosy said. "Monty thought so, too, which is why he helped him. I'm glad he did because Jacob is turning out to be a great help. If you want to catch his interest, ask him about cooking. I think it's his favorite subject, and he'd love to have his own restaurant one day."

"Thank you… I'll do that. Men love to talk about themselves, and the more we listen, the more they like us," Elizabeth giggled.

"You are right about that," Rosy agreed.

"Please tell me honestly how you are doing. Is there anything you need? Anything I can do?" Elizabeth asked.

Rosy shook her head. "I'll be all right. It'll take time, I'm sure, but I'll get through. Having friends is a great help. You can come and visit me here as often as you'd like."

"I will," Elizabeth promised. "I always wished for a big sister, and that's who you are to me."

Rosy hugged Elizabeth before she headed into the kitchen, and Elizabeth left for home.

As she walked down the boardwalk, she decided she was an adult, and as such, she should have some say in her life.

The first thing she would announce was that she wished to be called Beth. She'd inform her father that she wanted to teach and didn't want to be courted by whoever he found that he thought was worthy. At least she'd try to tell him. She doubted he'd listen, but no one could force her to be friendly to the men her father brought around. Truthfully, as long as her friends called her Beth, she'd be happy.

Elizabeth picked up her pace as she hurried home. She'd tell her mother first. Perhaps she might help her convince her father.

She ran up the stairs and pushed open the front door before the housekeeper could open it for her.

"Mother, I'm home," she called out.

"Elizabeth Rose Dubois, we do not shout," her mother reprimanded as Elizabeth bounded into the parlor.

"Perhaps Elizabeth Rose doesn't, but from this day forward, I'm Beth. I might consider Beth Rose, but the only time I will be Elizabeth is when I must sign my legal name, such as on a contract. I fully intend to go after the teacher's position. I also decided I will not be courted by the boring men Father plans to bring home to meet me. I will decide who I love and who I marry someday."

Elizabeth dropped onto the settee and smiled at her mother. Dorothea appeared pale and patted her chest.

"Don't worry, Mother. I can have the life I want without causing a scandal or embarrassing you and Father," Beth said.

"I certainly hope you do, and I would suggest waiting to tell your father until he's had at least one brandy. Two would be best," Dorothea advised.

Beth smiled.

As Elizabeth hurried home to try to convince her parents of her choices, Jacob was busy helping Rosy prepare supper for the diner customers. He was quiet as usual, but Rosy sensed he had something on his mind.

"Is something wrong, Jacob?" Rosy asked.

"No, I have a lot on my mind," Jacob answered as he checked the beef roast in the oven.

"Could part of what's on your mind be a lovely lady with blue eyes?" Rosy asked.

Jacob felt his face warm, but men don't blush. It was the heat from the oven. He hoped Rosy wouldn't notice.

"I'm not sure what you mean. I was thinking about a new beef roast recipe," Jacob lied.

"Uh-huh," Rosy said. "Beth is a lovely young woman. She's bright and friendly. She has a teaching certificate, but her heart is in business. She'd love to help run a business. I suppose she gets that from her father."

"That's a good thing. I wish her well," Jacob stammered while doing his best not to look at Rosy.

"You might want to speak to her about your future plans. I know they're only a dream right now, but her business sense might help you make plans," Rosy suggested. "You can never have too much knowledge when you're planning your future."

Jacob nodded. "I suppose you're right. If I get a chance to speak to Miss Beth, I will."

"I'm sure she'd appreciate that someone is interested in her mind and her thoughts. Her father's goal is to marry her off to some man who can help him build his financial empire and political aspirations," Rosy offered.

She knew getting the shy young man to share his feelings would be nearly impossible, but if she talked about Beth, she could plant a seed. They were perfect for each other. One shy, one forthright. One culinary-minded, one business-minded. Both sweet. What could possibly go wrong? She knew each was interested in the other, but Jacob needed a little push. Yes, she'd keep planting seeds.

CHAPTER 3

Two days after Elizabeth visited with Rosy and had a short conversation with Jacob Wheeler, her father sat his wife and daughter down to share some exciting news. At least he thought it was exciting.

"Dorothea, Elizabeth." Henry pursed his lips and brushed down the front of his shirt. "Mr. Henry Davenport will be having supper with us tonight. He's a very talented hatmaker in from Savannah, Georgia. He's looking to freight some of his merchandise to our town. I've been corresponding with him for a couple months now."

"Oh, splendid," said Mrs. Dubois. "Isn't that exciting, Elizabeth?" Her eyes flashed across the room to Edward. "Tell me, darlin', is he married?"

"Mother!" Elizabeth exclaimed. "You're incorrigible."

"Well, now that you ask, Dorothea," he said as he poured himself a brandy and picked up the glass. Smiling, he answered, "No, he's not married. And from the businesses he owns across the East, he's a very wealthy young man." He looked at Elizabeth and winked. "I want you to get gussied up in one of those pretty little dresses your mother bought you in New Orleans."

Elizabeth had all she could stand from both her mother and father.

She figured now was the time to let her thoughts be known about Jacob Wheeler. What she didn't realize was that her words would cause an avalanche of anger from her father.

"I don't want to eat supper with a stranger, Father. And I would rather you call me Beth from now on. I have never liked the name Elizabeth."

Dorothea put her hand to her chest. She had warned her daughter to wait until her father had consumed at least two glasses of brandy before having this conversation. But now that the cat was out of the bag, there was no way of putting it back.

"Let her talk, Dorothea. I've heard that young ladies go through periods of insanity. Sounds like Elizabeth has taken leave of her senses. Go ahead, my dear. Wax on. Wax on."

Elizabeth shook her head in anger but then quickly collected herself and spoke calmly. "Father, Mother, I do not want either of you promising me off to a man of your choosing. I'm not a piece of property or livestock to be bartered for. Now, I know that the two of you want the best for me, but I've got to make my own decisions."

"Are you finished, dear?" asked Mr. Dubois in a condescending tone as he poured himself a second glass of brandy. He stared at his daughter portentously and raised his glass to his wife as a toast. "To our spirited, independent daughter… who doesn't appreciate all that we've done for her."

"It's not that…"

Edward interrupted his daughter before she could finish. He raised his finger and yelled from across the room. "Now, let me tell you, young lady, what you're going to do!"

Dorothea stepped toward Edward, waving her hand. "Don't shout, Edward. Otherwise, the help will hear and talk about it among the townspeople."

"Yes," said Elizabeth, with her hands on her hips. "We wouldn't want our pristine image to be marred, now would we?"

Mr. Dubois lunged across the room. Standing just inches from Elizabeth, and through gritted teeth, he whispered, "Be ready by seven p.m. in the dress I told you to wear. And you best behave yourself tonight or I'll..." He raised his hand as if he would slap her.

"Edward!" said Dorothea in protest. "Please don't be so harsh with Elizabeth." This time, however, her concern was not about their house servants overhearing. She was genuinely concerned for her daughter's safety. Edward Dubois, she knew from personal experience, had a very serious and dangerous temper. In fact, he had raised his hand to her before—only one time—but she would never forget it. She touched her face, remembering the sting of his backhand.

Elizabeth put her hand to her mouth and ran upstairs to her room crying. Dorothea started to go after her when Edward grabbed her by the arm. "Let her go, honey." He pulled Dorothea into his arms and held her tightly, too tightly.

As she stood there in her husband's embrace, her mind traveled back twenty years to when she, like Elizabeth, was a strong, independent young woman. She also remembered how Edward was so kind and gentle when he was sparking her. *He promised my father he'd always be good to me, never harsh.* Now, she realized what a lie that had been. *He also said he'd never take me away from my family. That was a lie, too.*

Dorothea gently pushed away from Edward. A tear ran down her cheek. "I'll see what I can do to get Elizabeth to come around."

"That's my girl." He reached out and stroked her face. "We'll dine at Rosy's. For some reason, Davenport wants some down-home Texas cooking." Edward rolled his eyes and held his palms in the air. With a smirk, he asked, "Why would he want anything from Texas? These barbarians will never be civilized."

Dorothea went up to Elizabeth's room. She knocked on her door and slowly turned the knob to open it. "Honey, are you all right?"

"Yes, Mother, I am. But I am so angry right now, I could just spit." She balled her hand into a fist.

"Oh, Elizabeth," her mother said with a slight smile. "You do have a way with words, dear."

Both of them laughed, then Dorothea stepped over and joined Elizabeth on the side of her bed. She patted her on the hand. "This meeting tonight means a lot to your father. I'm sure if Mr. Davenport decides to do business in Palestine, your father will benefit financially."

"Mother, you know I love Father, but…"

"Elizabeth, do this for me, please?"

Elizabeth looked into her mother's eyes and noticed they were red. "Have you been crying, Ma?"

She waved her hand, dismissing the notion. "Of course not. Now, can I count on you to come with us to supper… in the dress your father requested?"

"All right, Mother. I'll go, but I'm not looking to wed Mr. Davenport or anybody else Father recommends. I have plans of my own, one of which is choosing my own husband."

LATE THAT AFTERNOON, Henry Davenport arrived in Palestine by train. Mayor Dubois was there at the depot to meet him in his barouche, drawn by two large, midnight black horses. "Welcome to Palestine, Mr. Davenport." Edward held out his hand.

Davenport touched his black cane to his derby, then shook Dubois' hand. "Thank you, kind sir."

"Grab his bags, Charley." Edward motioned to his driver. "I've made reservations for you at the hotel. I'm sure you'll want to rest up before supper."

"That I would, Mr. Dubois. That I would. Though the trip from Savannah was delightful, it was a bit taxing." Davenport stretched his arms in the air.

The two men climbed up into the carriage and made small talk while Charley loaded Davenport's bag, unhitched the team, and crawled up into the driver's seat. Gathering the reins, he clucked to the horses and they moved forward, pulling their freight.

As they pulled up in front of the hotel, Charley jumped down and opened the carriage door. Then, he hurried around to the back and collected Davenport's bags and carried them inside to the front desk.

"Well, Mr. Davenport, we will meet you here at the front door around seven. The diner is right around the corner... if you are still wanting some down-home Texas cooking."

"That I am, sir. Seven o'clock sounds splendid." Henry tipped his hat and went inside.

Edward rolled his eyes and barked, "Rattle your hocks, Charley. The sun is boiling my brain."

"Yes, sir," answered his driver. Within seconds, the carriage sped away up Main Street and back to Dubois' home.

As Edward entered the front door, Dorothea met him with a smile. "I see Mr. Davenport's train arrived on time. Would you like a brandy, dear?"

Edward smiled, "That I would, Dorothea," he said as he pulled off his hat and gloves and set them down on the narrow table next to the door.

"Have a seat, Edward. I'll bring it to you."

Dubois sat down in the plush, felt-covered chair and shifted around until he got comfortable. Then, he reached for his pipe, emptied the ashes into a silver tray, and opened a small canvas bag. The scent of cherry blend tobacco quickly filled the room. Edward inserted the small bowl of the pipe into the bag and tamped the chamber full of fresh tobacco. Putting the small hollow tip of the pipe to his lips, he lit a match and held it to the bowl, sucking the flame into the dark brown tobacco. It ignited, and the smoke wafted into the air.

Elizabeth could smell her father's burning pipe from her room. In the past, she had always liked the aroma. The cherry blend was her favorite. This evening, however, the odor of the pipe caused her to feel anxious. She knew that her father was home and that soon he would be expecting her to walk down the stairwell in one of the fancy dresses purchased by her mother to impress a stranger she was being forced to dine with.

Anger welled up within her as she sat and stared into the mirror and brushed her long brown hair. *I feel like a heifer about to be run through an auction. This, this aristocrat from Georgia. Who does he think he is? A glorified hatmaker. That means little to me.*

Dorothea brought Edward his brandy, then hurried upstairs to check on Elizabeth. One thing she knew her husband did not tolerate was tardiness. She gently knocked on Elizabeth's door.

"Come in, Mother." Beth knew from the knock that it was her.

Dorothea looked across the room and saw the lacy white dress Elizabeth had taken out of the closet and laid across her bed. "Oh, that is an excellent choice, Elizabeth. Your father will be so pleased."

"Is that our lot in life, Mother, to always try and please Father?"

"Elizabeth Rose. Now, what kind of question is that?"

Immediately, Elizabeth thought about the name her mother had just called her: Elizabeth Rose. In that moment, she thought of Rosy at the diner and thought, *that's just one more reason I like Rosy Baker.* Then, she felt the stare of her mother and asked, "What did you say, Mother?"

Dorothea shook her head in frustration. "I just don't know where your mind is these days, Elizabeth. You're not a child anymore."

"No, Mother, I'm not. Yet, I am constantly being treated like one." She stared over at the dress draped over the bed. "Wear this, young lady. Go here. Act this way. You and Father treat me as if I'm a child."

Suddenly, the door to her room flung open, banging against the dresser next to it. Standing in the threshold was Edward and his eyes were ablaze with anger. He pulled his belt from the loop of his pants and warned, "You're not too old to get a lashing." Dorothea stepped in front of Edward and pleaded with him to calm down. He pushed her aside and pointed across the room. "This is your last warning, Elizabeth. I'll not tolerate your insubordination."

He aggressively reached into his vest pocket and pulled out his watch. "We leave in thirty minutes. Don't make us late."

As he turned to walk out, he saw the white dress and stopped. Suddenly, his demeanor changed. Turning on his heels, he said, "Aw, that's a lovely choice, my dear." With a large smile, he backed out of the door and eased it closed.

Elizabeth's mouth hung open as she and her mother looked at one another. Neither said a word for the next few moments. Then, Dorothea walked over to her daughter, took the brush from her hand,

and stroked her hair. "You have the prettiest hair, Elizabeth. I've always enjoyed brushing it. My mother wouldn't let me grow out my hair, you know? And your father, well, he's always demanded I keep it this length." She put her hand to the back of her head, to the length of her hair.

Elizabeth studied her mother's face in the mirror and at that moment, for the first time in her life, felt sorry for her. *Poor Mother. She just does what Father tells her to do without a thought of her own. He's so manipulative, so cruel. I can't wait to leave here and be on my own.*

Dorothea smiled. "There now." She set the brush down and kissed the top of Elizabeth's head. "Your hair is shining like silk. You will be the most beautiful woman in Palestine tonight."

As she started toward the door, Elizabeth reached out and took her by the arm.

"The second prettiest woman, Mother."

Dorothea waved her hand and smiled, dismissing her daughter's words. But Elizabeth didn't stop. She stood and pulled her mother toward her. "Sit down and let me brush your hair."

"What? No, no. We must get ready." She hurried toward the door. For some reason, Dorothea had never been one to show much affection. It always seemed to make her uncomfortable.

Thirty minutes passed by quickly, and Elizabeth made sure she was ready ahead of time. As she walked down the stairwell of their two-story home, Edward, who was dressed in his finest suit, was standing at the bottom of the stairs with his hand out.

Elizabeth plastered on a smile, pulled up the bottom of her dress, and slowly made her way down. "You look lovely, my dear." Edward took her hand and kissed it. Then, he gave her a whirl.

Dorothea clapped from the top of the stairs. "Oh, Elizabeth, you are simply beautiful."

Elizabeth turned to her father. "Look how wonderful Mother looks. Isn't she ravishing?"

Edward stared up and, with a slight smile, said, "Why, yes. Dorothea, you look ravishing."

She smiled and pulled up on her dress to take the first step down.

Edward turned to the door dismissively and said, "Hurry along now. We have a guest waiting." He walked briskly out of the room.

Elizabeth saw the disappointment in her mother's eyes. Looking back to the door, then up to Dorothea, she began to clap. "Your carriage awaits you, beautiful lady."

Edward heard the commotion and stepped back into the house. "Let's go," he barked angrily.

The ride to the hotel was a short one. Nobody said a word. Elizabeth was still seething over her father's inattentiveness to her mother, a pattern she was noticing more and more in the last few hours.

As they pulled up in front of the hotel, Henry Davenport stepped outside. Charley climbed down and opened the carriage door. Edward stepped down and held his hand out for Dorothea. Right behind her was Elizabeth.

"Well, Mr. Dubois, I must say…" He tipped his hat. "I am jealous of the beauty that surrounds your travel. Who are these lovely ladies?"

Edward smiled with satisfaction. "This is my wife, Dorothea."

Davenport took Dorothea's hand and kissed it. "I am delighted to meet you, Mrs. Dubois."

She curtsied and said, "Likewise, Mr. Davenport.

"And this is my daughter, Elizabeth Rose."

Davenport tipped his hat and took her by the hand. Kissing it, he said, "It is my pleasure to meet you, Miss Elizabeth Rose."

Elizabeth curtsied and said, "Well, thank you, Mr. Davenport."

"Oh please, call me Henry," he said as he stared at Elizabeth.

Edward cleared his throat. "Well, shall we proceed to the diner?"

"Diner?" asked Elizabeth, abruptly.

"Yes, dear," said Edward with a look of reprimand. "Rosy's Diner."

Elizabeth chuckled nervously, and her eyes darted back and forth from her father to Henry. "Father, are you sure Mr. Davenport wouldn't prefer something a little more upscale? Rosy's Diner is a meat-and-potatoes kind of place." Beth wasn't really that concerned about their guest's preference, she just didn't want to go into Rosy's looking as if she had a date, especially in front of Jacob.

CHAPTER 4

Beth silently fumed, wondering why of all the places, her father would choose the diner. Did he know she was attracted to Jacob? No, he couldn't. Did he have spies watching her? No, he wouldn't, or would he? It didn't matter. She liked Jacob, and her father would have to learn to live with that fact.

Arriving at the diner, Henry held the door for Dorothea, Beth, and the mayor. Rosy, surprised to see a formal group enter the diner, hurried over to welcome them.

"Good evening, Mister Mayor, Missus Dubois, and Beth. I have a nice table for the four of you near the windows."

Henry made sure he helped Beth take her seat and took the chair across from her. The mayor was ready to sit when he realized his wife was still standing. He walked around the table and helped her to sit before taking his chair.

Rosy said, "I'll have coffee and tea brought to the table immediately while you decide what you'd like for supper. Steak, fried potatoes, and green beans is tonight's special."

Beth gave Rosy a withering smile, and Rosy nodded her understanding. The diner was the last place Rosy expected to see Beth dressed in a formal white gown. It would have better suited her for a night at the theater.

Jacob brought four white cups to the table and greeted the guests. "Good evening, Missus Dubois, Miss Beth, and Mister Mayor."

Mayor Dubois raised his voice and nearly shouted, "How dare you address my daughter as Beth. Her name is Elizabeth Rose, but to you, young man, she is Miss Dubois. I hope I'm making myself clear."

"Umm, yes, sir, Mister Mayor. I understand," Jacob stammered before hurrying off.

Beth glared at her father. "It was unfair to take your anger out on Jacob. He's my friend, and I asked him to call me Beth. All my friends call me Beth."

"Your name is Elizabeth Rose, and as long as you live under my roof, you will be addressed properly by the riff-raff in this town," her father growled.

He turned to Henry and said, "I apologize. Small town people have small minds at times. You must excuse their ill manners, but their money is as good as anyone's, and business does well here."

Henry nodded. "I understand, sir."

Before he could continue, Beth interrupted. "Father, I'm twenty-two, and I can decide what I wish to be called. I chose Beth."

"No one named Beth will reside under my roof," the mayor insisted.

"Then, perhaps," Beth answered, "it's time I find somewhere else to live."

Dorothea gasped. "Elizabeth, this is not the place to discuss such matters and certainly not in front of Mr. Davenport. We'll discuss this at home."

"There will be no discussion," the mayor insisted. "Henry might as well know now that Elizabeth can be strongheaded, but with the right man, her will can be tamed and used for good."

Elizabeth's temper boiled, and she spat, "The way you've tamed Mother's?"

Elizabeth turned to Henry and added, "If my father invited you here to meet me as part of some marriage business deal, you must know I'm not getting married until I decide I want to and then only to a man of my choosing."

Rosy chose that minute to come to the table with a metal coffee pot and white china teapot, asking who would prefer tea and who preferred coffee.

Beth smiled and said, "Tea, please, Rosy, and Mother prefers tea, as well."

"Gentlemen?" Rosy asked.

Coffee was the answer from both men, and after Rosy filled their cups, she asked if they were ready to order.

Mayor Dubois looked at Henry, and he said, "I'd like something Western."

Beth bit back a smile, and Rosy answered, "I can bring you a steak with beans and tortillas."

"I'd like to try that," Henry said.

Mayor Dubois spoke up. "My wife, daughter, and I will have the special."

Beth's ire rose again when she heard her father order for her—he knew full well that she didn't care for steak. She looked at Rosy and proclaimed, "Rosy, I'll have the chicken and dumplings."

Rosy nodded, Mayor Dubois scowled at Beth, and Dorothea paled, waiting for her husband to embarrass himself and the family in public. She waited, but Edward remained quiet before turning to Henry and asking him about his business plans.

Beth knew a battle waited at home, and she knew, if necessary, she would leave. Her father ignored the fact that she was a wealthy young woman in her own right and could make her own way. Her maternal grandfather had left her a substantial inheritance, which she had received while at the teacher's college.

Her grandfather had disliked her father and left a provision in his will that Beth's inheritance was not to be touched by her father for any reason. Beth's attorney passed the documentation on to the bank when she first received her inheritance, and the instructions were on file now in the local bank there. Beth didn't trust her father's influence and left most of her inheritance in a St. Louis bank before coming to Palestine.

Beth was lost in her thoughts when Jacob arrived at the table with heaping plates for Dorothea and her.

As he placed the plates on the table, he said, "Enjoy your suppers Missus Dubois, Miss Dubois."

Beth smiled her best smile at Jacob and said, "Thank you, Jacob. I'm sure we will."

Her father scowled at her again and at Jacob when he returned with his and Henry's suppers.

Beth bowed her head in prayer and said grace before picking up her fork. When she lifted her head, she saw Henry staring at her.

"Is something wrong, Henry?" Beth asked.

"No, I thought you might be ill."

"I was praying," Beth replied.

A quick laugh shook Henry's shoulders, and he grimaced. "I suppose people do that."

Beth's mouth dropped open, but she shut it quickly. How could her father expect this man to be a proper suitor for her? She'd never marry a man who scoffed at her beliefs.

The mayor ignored his daughter's obvious displeasure with Henry and instead started a conversation with him about the future of his business in Palestine.

Beth looked at her mother and rolled her eyes. Dorothea answered with a small, strained smile. It would be a long, uncomfortable supper.

Beth's appetite dissipated with Henry's attitude, but she loved Rosy's chicken and dumplings, so she began eating. Besides, the last thing she wanted to do was have her father find another reason to belittle her. Not eating the supper she had insisted on would certainly give him a reason.

Rosy stopped by the table to ask how they were enjoying their meal.

Henry never even looked up as he shoveled more beans into his mouth.

Mayor Dubois simply nodded.

Dorothea smiled, and Beth told Rosy she had outdone herself once again.

As the men discussed business, Beth and her mother ate their suppers in silence. Beth knew her father brought them along as window dressing. There was no need for her to be there, especially dressed the way she was.

She glanced toward the kitchen several times, catching Jacob's eye twice. Finally, he smiled, and she tried to smile just enough so Jacob would know she was returning his smile but not broadly enough for her father to disapprove.

When they finished supper, Jacob quickly removed the dishes, and Rosy arrived with plates of fresh apple pie. Henry dug in as if he were starving, and Beth laughed to herself, wondering if she obeyed her father and married someone like Henry, how she would ever keep up feeding the man.

Jacob walked up to the table and asked if they needed anything else and if he could remove their pie plates. Everyone nodded except Beth, who smiled and said, "Yes, Jacob, thank you."

As Jacob gathered the plates, he smiled back and said, "You're welcome, Miss Dubois."

Beth smiled again. "Will we see you at church on Sunday? There is a social afterward."

"I believe so. Rosy is baking pies for the social, and the diner will be closed," Jacob explained.

"Wonderful," Beth replied. "I'll see you there."

Then, she winked at him. Jacob's face began to redden, and the mayor's squinted eyes told him to leave their table immediately.

"What was all that about?" the mayor asked.

"What?" Beth asked, shrugging one shoulder.

"You shouldn't be speaking to that man. We invited Henry to be our guest, and you've ignored him," Mayor Dubois said angrily to his daughter.

Beth tried to smile. "Jacob is a friend. I hardly know Mr. Davenport. Besides, he seems too busy eating to hold a conversation."

Her father's glare told Beth she was going too far, but she no longer cared. After seeing Jacob and Henry together, she realized they were far different men, and if one would win her heart, it would be Jacob Wheeler.

Mayor Dubois left money on the table for their bill and stood. Henry nearly tripped as he rushed around the table to help Beth stand. Dorothea sat patiently while Edward spoke to Henry for a moment before attending to her and helping her stand.

Rosy hurried to the table and asked if they enjoyed their meal.

Beth, not waiting to give her father the chance to say a word, said, "It was delicious, as always." She reached out and hugged Rosy, and Rosy returned the hug. "I'll see you soon," Beth promised.

Henry agreed with Beth. "The meal was quite interesting. I did enjoy the beans and tortillas, and you do make an excellent pie."

Mayor Dubois remained quiet as he escorted his wife to the door.

Henry offered Beth his arm. She couldn't do anything except slip her arm in his, but she made sure to stop and wave at Jacob before they left.

On the stroll back to the hotel, Henry asked Beth if she'd have supper with him at the hotel the following evening. Beth apologized and said that she had another engagement since she was helping with the arrangements for the church social. It was only a partial lie because she was on the committee but, truthfully, she would be free by suppertime. She silently asked God to forgive her lie and to help her out of the situation with Henry.

"Another time, then?" Henry asked. "I will be in town for a while. Your father is quite the businessman, not to mention he seems to make a good mayor. Everyone I spoke to has praised his good sense."

Beth wanted to laugh, wondering who in town would be brave enough to say anything disparaging against Edward Dubois.

"Yes, he is good at business, and another time would be delightful. Thank you," Beth said as they approached the front doors of the hotel.

Henry said his good nights and kissed Beth's hand before entering the hotel.

Beth waited for her father's anger, but it didn't appear on the carriage ride or once they arrived home. Instead, Edward disappeared into his office and shut the door behind him.

Beth sighed and asked her mother, "Do you suppose Father is angry enough with me not to discuss supper, or will he speak to me later?"

Dorothea took Beth's hands and said, "You worry too much about your father's temper. He may try to frighten you at times, but he would never hurt you."

"But has he hurt you, Mother?"

"Not intentionally. Now, run off to bed before you ruin that lovely dress," Dorothea said, before turning and walking into the parlor.

Beth did as her mother suggested and hurried upstairs before her father finished in his office.

～

BETH SPENT the afternoon with the ladies on the church social planning committee but finished well before suppertime. She walked behind the stores and hotel on the main street, hoping to avoid Henry, and prayed her father wouldn't bring the man home with him.

Mayor Dubois arrived late for supper as usual. Their cook had learned not to say a word and do her best to keep the meal hot without burning it.

Dorothea sat patiently waiting while Beth's leg bounded up and down under the table. A stern look from her mother had Beth sitting up, straight and quiet.

"Good evening, ladies," the mayor said as he entered the room, brushing a quick kiss on his wife's cheek, and taking his place at the head of the table.

Beth raised her eyebrows and glanced at her mother. Dorothea gave a slight shake of her head, and Beth knew not to say a word.

When Edward finished his meal and set his fork down, he cleared his throat and said, "Elizabeth, I understand you turned down a supper invitation with Henry because you had a previous engagement. Yet, here you sit with your mother and me."

"I thought I'd be busy through supper since I had a meeting with the ladies from church," Beth explained.

The mayor nodded. "I suppose you must do that to keep up appearances. It wouldn't do to have the mayor's daughter ignore responsibilities. We must show our best face in town. I do want to win the next election. First, however, you should accept Henry's invitation. He's successful and will only continue to be when he opens his hat shop here in town."

Beth took a deep breath and said, "I don't care for Mr. Davenport. I would prefer not to have supper with him."

"There is nothing wrong with Henry Davenport. However, your behavior last night was not proper. He's new in town and only wanted to enjoy a Texas meal."

"He scoffed at me for saying grace," Beth retorted.

"Everyone worships in his own way. I suppose you would prefer to have supper with that man who cleans tables and dishes at the diner?" the mayor asked.

"Yes, I would. Jacob is my friend, and I enjoy his company."

The mayor sat quietly, and Beth watched his hands ball into fists, knowing his anger was growing.

"Elizabeth Rose Dubois, I forbid you to see or speak to that reprobate. He crawled into town after most likely hopping a train, and the best he can do is wash dishes at the diner," the mayor shot back.

Beth answered, "He has plans for his future, and I think he will do well."

The mayor glared at his daughter and asked, "How well do you know this man?"

"Not well," Beth answered. "Rosy told me about his future plans."

"That's another thing," Mayor Dubois said, raising his index finger for emphasis, "I don't want you to associate with Rosy or anyone from the diner."

"Rosy is a good woman. She would be married to Sheriff Peel right now if he hadn't been killed," Beth defended her friend.

"I won't hear another word. I have made my decision, and you will abide by it," her father insisted.

"I won't," Beth argued. "I'm twenty-two and can do whatever I wish."

"I told you before, you will do as I say as long as you live under my roof!" Edward bellowed and hit the table with the flat of his hand.

Beth stood, "Then, I'll move. Right now. I'll go upstairs and pack."

Dorothea gasped and pleaded, "Edward, please don't argue with Beth. I don't want her to leave."

Edward scoffed. "She won't leave. Where would she go?"

Beth walked to the far end of the table and addressed her parents, "I'm sorry, Mother, but I can't live like this any longer. Father, you know I have money from Grandfather's estate."

"Yes, you do," he growled. "I also know the bank president and I am the mayor of Palestine. So, who do you think he'll listen to?"

Beth drew in a breath. "He'll listen to the law. Grandfather didn't trust you. My inheritance comes with a provision that you have no control whatsoever over it."

Mayor Dubois laughed. "Do you think that will stop me? One note from me tonight, and you won't have money in the bank tomorrow."

"Grandfather expected that, and his lawyer has the bulk of my estate safely deposited in several banks. You can't get to them all, Father."

Beth turned on her heel and left her sobbing mother and fuming father in the dining room. Hurrying to her room, Beth reached into the drawer that held her personal items and found the small cloth bag that held enough cash to see her through several months. Her lawyer had suggested that she keep emergency cash on hand, and she was pleased that she had listened.

Not knowing what her father might do, Beth took the small bag and tied the string tightly to the strap of her camisole. Then, she adjusted her dress so that the bag was invisible. She threw enough clothes in a carpetbag to get her through a few days and stopped to say a prayer.

Asking for God's guidance, Beth picked up the carpetbag and walked down the stairs.

Her mother was still sitting at the dining room table while her father stood stoically at the head of the table.

"If you leave, you are not welcome to come back," he said.

"I know," Beth replied sadly. "But I need to live a life I can be proud of and not cower to anyone."

"You'll never get that teaching position," he threatened.

Beth shrugged. "Palestine isn't the only town that needs teachers."

Before her father could say another word, Beth hurried out the front door, walking briskly toward town.

CHAPTER 5

Elizabeth went straight to Rosy's house, three streets up from her home, and sat her bag down at the door. Then, she eased into the chair on the porch and waited. She knew Rosy would be working late at the diner and didn't want to bother her.

About an hour later, Beth heard a familiar voice. "Why, Beth Dubois, what in the world are you doing out here at this time of night?" Jacob was accompanying Rosy as he usually did when they closed the diner at night. He stood, silently waiting for Beth's response.

"I've moved out of my parent's house and was wondering if I could stay here for the night. Then, tomorrow I will check with Mrs. Downing at the boarding house for a room."

"Why, sure, Beth, you are welcome to stay here tonight. Do you think you ought to let your mother and father know where you are, so they won't worry?"

Elizabeth shook her head aggressively and rose to her feet. "No, Rosy, I don't. I'm tired of being treated like a child." Then, she looked over the rail at Jacob, who stood in the shadows in silence. "Jacob, I owe you an apology for my father's rude behavior tonight. And, as for that Mr. Davenport, who I was sitting across from… that, too, was my father's doing."

Jacob didn't know what to say. He stepped forward and removed his hat. "I'm sorry, Miss Dubois—I mean, Beth—that you're having to go through this. It sure took a lot of courage for you to leave your parents' house."

Rosy stared at Jacob, hoping he would rush forward and put his arm around Beth, but he didn't. *What am I going to do with that boy? I know good and well he loves Beth, and tonight would be a good night for him to tell her.* Then, she sighed. *Who am I fooling? He's just like Monty, a typical man afraid to show his feelings.*

Beth stared down at the wooden planks on Rosy's porch. Then, she raised her head. "Thank you, Jacob, for your kind words and Rosy for letting me stay the night." She reached and picked up her bag. "If you've got a room for me, I'd sure like to go to it. I'm afraid I'm quite weary from the confrontation with my father. A good night of sleep will refresh me and hopefully, clear my head."

Jacob took Beth's words as an invitation for him to leave. He put his hand to his hat, "Ladies, I will say good night. Rosy, I'll see you in the morning."

Rosy nodded and stepped to the door. "This way, dear." She opened the door and waved her hand in front of her.

Beth stepped toward her, but suddenly turned on her heels. "Good night, Jacob," she said with a warm smile.

"Good night, Beth," he said, with his signature grin, feeling closer now to Beth than he ever had. He could completely relate to the tension she was experiencing with her father, having experienced much of it with his own father before leaving home.

Jacob stood there until Rosy closed the door. Then, he proceeded down the boardwalk to Monty's house, the place he was currently staying since Monty's death. As he reached to turn the knob on the door, he felt someone grab him by the back of the shirt. A big man slung him around and into the wall. Then, another clubbed him over the head with an axe handle. A third man hit him in the lower back with a singletree.

Jacob slumped down to his knees, barely conscious, but his attackers didn't stop. They picked him up and dragged him into an alley where they took turns hitting him high and low as if his body were a punching bag. Wheeler managed to get in a couple punches of his own, but the three men were just too strong for him.

"Stay away from Elizabeth Dubois or we'll kill you." Those were the last words Jacob remembered hearing before everything went dark and he passed out.

∽

BACK AT MS. Baker's house, Rosy tapped on Beth's door. "Beth, dear, just wanted to make sure you have everything you need."

Beth opened the door. "Yes, Rosy, thank you."

"Well, try to get a good night's rest. Things will look better in the morning," Rosy said with a gentle pat on her shoulder. Then, she turned to go to her room.

"Rosy," said Beth. "Do you have a minute to talk?"

"Why, certainly, dear."

Beth pulled open the door and turned toward the bed. Both ladies sat down on the edge of it as Rosy reached and patted Beth's hand. "Now, tell Rosy what's on your mind."

Beth began to tell her about the last few weeks of her life and how she and her father had argued. "I love my mother and father, Rosy, but there's a lot of pretension going on."

"Pretension, dear?"

"Yes. Father is not what he appears to be in public. He came to Palestine with political ambitions. He hopes to be a Texas senator in the near future. Of course, nobody knows that but mother and me."

Rosy wanted to comfort Elizabeth but felt a bit uneasy with the personal information she was disclosing. "Maybe I shouldn't be hearing this, dear. Your father..."

"Oh, but Rosy, I have no one else to confide in. You saw the way Father treated me at the diner tonight. He all but had me married off to Henry Davenport, the hatmaker from Georgia."

"So, that's who he is. Jacob and I wondered. Your pa never did actually introduce him." She nudged Elizabeth's elbow. "I do believe Mr. Wheeler was a mite jealous of your beau."

Beth sighed as she cocked her head sideways and stared over at Rosy. "Like I said, Henry is not my beau. Father just insisted that I put on a new dress and join them for supper."

"And a pretty dress it was, dear." She winked at Beth. "I do believe Jacob liked it, too. Why, he couldn't keep his eyes off you."

"Really, Rosy?" she said, with excitement in her voice. She sat up straight on the bed and asked, "But why do you say that?"

"Well, honey, I am a woman." Rosy touched her chest. "And women notice such things. Jacob Wheeler doesn't know it yet, but he's in love with you."

Rosy's observation made Elizabeth smile as wide as the Rio Grande. She jumped up from the bed and gave her host a huge hug. "You've made my night, Rosy. That's the best news I've heard in a long time." Then, Beth stepped back and said in a serious tone, "I just hope you're right about Jacob."

Reaching out with her hand, she took Elizabeth's hand in hers. "Give him some time. He's a typical man, you know, slow about things such as… love. Fact is, Sheriff Peel was the same way. Didn't think the man would ever say he loved me. But he did, and so will Jacob. I'm sure of it. Now, what do you say the both of us get a good night's sleep?"

Elizabeth nodded and pulled off her outer robe, laying it over a nearby chair. Rosy pulled back the covers on her bed and said good night.

For the next two hours, Beth lay there, looking up at the ceiling. She could not keep her heart from racing. She thought back over the confrontation she'd had with her father at the diner and then back at home. Although proud of herself for standing up to her father and claiming her independence, the prospect of being on her own was starting to settle in.

However, more pleasant thoughts quickly crowded out her anxiousness as her mind turned to Jacob Wheeler and the things Rosy had said about him, especially that she believed the young man was in love with her.

～

THE NEXT MORNING, Rosy arrived at the diner. Oddly, the back door was still locked, and the double cast-iron stoves had not been fired, two things Jacob Wheeler did the first thing he arrived every morning. Immediately, she knew something was wrong. Jacob Wheeler had never been late for work since the day he started. She feared the worst.

Running up the boardwalk, Rosy reached the sheriff's office. Pounding on the door, she woke up the new sheriff, Woodrow Wright.

"Hold your horses." Wright turned the knob on the door as he yelled, "Who in the Sam Hill is it?" When he looked up and saw that it was Rosy Baker, he stammered and said, "Oh, pardon me, ma'am."

"Sheriff Wright!" exclaimed Rosy. "Something is wrong. You know Jacob Wheeler, the young man that helps me in the diner?"

"Yes, ma'am. I know who you're talking about." He rubbed the sleep from his eyes.

"He's not at work this morning. He's never once been late. The last time I saw him was last night around nine o'clock when he walked me home. Please. Please, help me find him."

"Why sure, Miss Rosy. Let me grab my gun and hat and I'll be right with you. Would you care to come in?"

"No, thank you, Sheriff. I'll wait out here, but please hurry."

Lep came to the door and stared up at Rosy. "Well, hey, boy," Rosy said as she patted the hound on the head.

Wright was inside pulling on his boots, buckling on his gun, and grabbing his hat. Then, he pulled the door back open and said, "Let's see if we can find Jacob, ma'am. Maybe he just slept in late this morning."

Rosy hoped that was the case, but deep in her chest was a gnawing worry that something bad had befallen him.

Sheriff Wright and Rosy arrived at Monty's house and pounded away on the door. Jacob didn't answer. Rosy's feelings of foreboding grew with each unanswered knock. She put her hand to her chest.

Woodrow reached and turned the knob. Pushing through the door, he and Rosy called out as each stepped inside, "Jacob, Jacob. Are you in here?" Given that Monty Peel's house was only a one room lean-to, with just a glance they knew Wheeler wasn't there.

As they stepped back out on the stoop, Wright surveilled up and down the street. Then, his eyes turned to one of the alleys nearby. Call it a premonition, lawman instinct, or perhaps the hand of God, but something told him to check it out. "I'll be right back, Miss Rosy."

Rosy sat down on the steps leading up to Monty's door and began to pray silently. *Lord, please help us find Jacob. I fear he needs our help.* She lowered her head into her hands, which were in her lap.

The sheriff had just left her to cross the street when he called out, "Miss Rosy!"

When she looked up, she saw a man staggering out of the alley. His whole face was covered in blood as he clenched his side with his hand.

"Jacob!" yelled Rosy as she jumped to her feet and ran toward him.

Sheriff Wright was now just a couple of feet from him when Jacob fell forward into his arms. "I've got you, son," Woodrow said as he took hold of him and laid him flat on his back.

Rosy rushed to his side while Wright yelled, "Somebody get the doc."

"Oh, Jacob." She stroked his face. Her fingers rubbed across the dried, crusted blood of the multiple cuts covering his forehead and cheeks. "It looks as if someone tried to kill him." She stared up at Wright with angry eyes.

Woodrow, feeling helpless standing over the wounded man, knelt and scooped Jacob up in his arms and rushed him over to the jail where he set him down on his personal bunk. Rosy followed closely behind. Her emotions ran to and fro from serious worry for Jacob's life then to anger at whoever did this to her friend.

More and more people were moving now along the streets of Palestine. A crowd was starting to form outside the jail.

Elizabeth awoke, got dressed, and poured herself a cup of coffee from the pot Rosy had left on the stove. Then, she opened the door and stepped out onto the porch to welcome a new day.

As she sat down in the chair she had occupied last night, she took a sip of her coffee then saw two people up the street yelling and running. Then, she saw another and another. Stepping inside, she quickly dressed herself and decided to see what all the commotion was about.

Locking the door behind her, she left Rosy's at a quick pace. Two streets up she turned the corner and saw a dozen or more people crowded around the door of the jail. Then, suddenly, she saw Rosy step through the mob with her hand to the side of her face. Even from a distance, Beth could tell her friend was upset. Something was dreadfully wrong.

In that moment, Beth's heart skipped a beat. She knew then that something had happened to Jacob. Running across the street, she screamed, "Rosy, Rosy. Is Jacob all right?"

Rosy threw up her arms and stopped Beth from going any farther. Wiping the tears from her eyes and clearing her throat, Rosy spoke firmly. "Beth, Jacob has been badly injured."

"What? What happened?" she asked frantically. "Did he get burned? Did he get cut?" She tried to understand what might have befallen him in the kitchen. "What happened to him, Rosy?"

"It looks as if someone tried to kill him. They beat him unmercifully. The doctor said one of his arms is broken, three ribs are busted, and…"

"And what?!" yelled Beth as she stared over Rosy's shoulder to the door of the jail. "What?"

"He's in a coma. His eyes are closed, and he hasn't said anything since he staggered out of that alley over there and the sheriff carried him to his office."

"I've got to see him, Rosy." Beth took off toward the jail, but Rosy caught her by the arm.

"Beth, Beth—listen to me. I don't think it's a good idea to see him the way he is. His face is so swollen from the beating that you won't recognize him. Maybe you should wait a few days and then come back."

"Rosy Baker," Beth said with a wrinkled face as she pointed. "If that was Monty Peel lying in there, wouldn't you want to see him? Wouldn't you *demand* to see him?"

Smiling, Rosy answered, "I sure would, Beth. You mind if I go with you?"

Holding one another's hands, the two women pushed their way through the crowd and pounded on the door. Sheriff Wright pulled it open and with an angry face started to say something until he saw that it was Rosy with the young Dubois woman.

"Ladies," he said, confused as to why Rosy was back and accompanied by Elizabeth.

"Sheriff Wright. This is Elizabeth Dubois, the mayor's daughter. We would like to see Jacob. We won't be but a minute."

Wright looked over his shoulder for the doc's permission. The doctor nodded, and Woodrow quickly ushered them on in, closing the door to the crowd still hanging around at the stoop.

As Beth walked toward the bunk that Jacob was lying on, a man in the corner stepped forward and stopped her in her tracks. It was her father, Edward Dubois, and he wore a strange grin on his face. "Elizabeth, honey. What are you doing here?" He stepped toward her and took her by the arm, but she quickly shook loose from his grip.

"I've come to see Jacob. How is he, Doctor?" she asked, ignoring her father's presence.

Edward stepped aside and answered, "Not too well, I'm afraid. Isn't that right, Doc?"

Sheriff Wright stood a few feet away, observing the strange behavior of the mayor, especially toward his daughter.

Rosy stared back toward the sheriff and crossed her arms. She, too, took note of Dubois' odd behavior.

As Beth stepped closer, the doctor moved away from Jacob's side.

That's when she saw the full extent of his injuries. She gasped. "Oh, my Lord. No."

Rosy stepped closer to her friend and placed her hand on her shoulder.

"Miss Baker, would you be so kind as to take Elizabeth Rose out of here? I don't think this is the proper place for her." Edward motioned toward the door.

His words grated on Beth's nerves. Suddenly, she regained her composure and knelt by Jacob's bedside. Stroking his face, she whispered, "We'll find the men who did this to you, Jacob." Then, she looked up to her father with eyes of suspicion. "Won't we, Mayor Dubois?"

"Miss Baker," said Edward as he gestured for her to take Beth out.

"I'll be happy to, Mr. Mayor, when Beth is good and ready."

"Very well," Dubois said. "Sheriff, I want you to find the men who did this. The town of Palestine will not tolerate this kind of violence, especially against an innocent young man such as Mr. Wheeler here. I'm offering a two hundred dollar reward for any information leading to their arrest."

CHAPTER 6

Beth glared at her father when he offered a two hundred dollar reward for the capture of the man or men who attacked Jacob. As usual, he was doing his best to make himself the center of attention.

Beth walked past him to get closer to Jacob, but he grabbed her arm.

"This is no place for you to be, Elizabeth. Go home. Your mother worried all night about you," the mayor said.

"I told you I was never coming home. I'm sorry that Mother is upset, but this is my life now," Beth said, trying to break her father's grip on her arm.

He dug his thumb into her arm, and she winced in pain. "I said go home. You're not to associate with this riff-raff. Stay in your room until I come home."

Beth yanked her arm free and stated, "I have a new home, and no one, not even you, can force me to go back to live with you and Mother. Your behavior when you grabbed my arm proves that I'm safer and will be happier living elsewhere."

Beth pushed past the mayor and moved closer to Jacob's side again.

"Remember," the mayor shouted over the concerned voices in the room, "that reward is two hundred dollars to the first person who brings me or the sheriff the name of the person or persons responsible for this heinous act."

Beth ignored her father and asked Dr. Reeves, "Is there anything I can do to help?"

Doc shook his head. "He's badly injured. I'm going to have him taken to my office so my wife and I can care for him properly."

"Surely," Beth pleaded, "there must be something."

"Pray," Doc answered. "He needs all our prayers now."

Beth stood back as a young man came rushing in carrying an old canvas stretcher.

"I want four men to place him as gently as possible on that stretcher and then carry him slowly back to my office. We can't take the chance of putting him in the back of a wagon. There are too many holes and rocks in the street. Don't jostle him and walk slowly and carefully," Reeves instructed, before leaving to ready his office for Jacob's arrival.

Jacob looked as if he were asleep, even with his battered and bruised face. Beth prayed he'd wake up knowing full well that a man beaten as badly as Jacob had been could easily succumb to his injuries.

Rosy placed her arm around Beth's shoulders. "Come on, I need to open the diner, and you can help. It'll keep your mind off what's happening."

Beth looked at Rosy with tears streaming down her cheeks and said, "Nothing will do that."

Rosy nodded. "All right, at least I can keep you busy. We're late for the breakfast rush, and people will want lunch soon. After lunch, we'll close the diner for a while and go see how Jacob is doing."

Beth nodded, and the two women headed for the diner.

Rosy said, "Let's keep the closed sign up until I can fry some bacon and sausage. No steaks this morning. We don't have enough time. We can offer bacon, sausage, eggs, and toast. I didn't have time to make biscuits."

"I can make the biscuits," Beth offered.

Rosy smiled. "You can cook?"

Beth put her hands to her hips and blinked her eyes rapidly. "Yes, I certainly can. When we lived in New Orleans, I visited my grandmother on weekends before she passed, and she taught me. She said every woman should learn how to cook. She used to tell me I might not marry as well as Mother did and should learn how to keep my husband happy," Beth offered, and smiled at the memory of the elderly grandmother she dearly loved.

"Well, I declare," said Rosy warmly. They were in the back kitchen now, getting ready to prep breakfast. She pointed to a cabinet. "You'll find what you need in there."

Beth slipped a clean white apron over her dark pink dress and said, "I need to stop at Mother's and speak to her about the rest of my things. This is the dress I wore at supper last night before I left. It's a bit dressy and cumbersome for work in the kitchen."

"You can do that when we close for lunch. I think today is going to be a simple cooking day. No stews or chicken and dumplings that take a while to cook. We'll feed them steaks and roast beef sandwiches for supper," Rosy suggested.

As Beth began making the biscuit dough, she asked Rosy, "I need to talk to someone about my worries. If I tell you what's on my mind, can you help me decide what to do?"

"Of course," Rosy answered as she waved a hand in the air. "You're like my little sister. You can always talk to me. Is this something you can't share with your mother?"

Beth gasped. "Heavens no, I could never tell Mother… but Rosy, I am almost certain that my father is behind Jacob's attack."

Suddenly, things got very quiet. Rosy stopped turning the sausages and stared in horror at Beth. "That's a terrible thing to say about your father. Are you sure? I know he's difficult, but he was trying to be helpful this morning."

Beth shook her head. "No, he wasn't. He was drawing attention to himself as always. He grabbed my arm, and it hurt badly enough that I'm sure I have a bruise. He looked into my eyes and told me to go home and stay away from the riff-raff in town. Last night he said he considered Jacob riff-raff and forbade me to see him. I refused and left home."

Rosy blew out a breath. "I was trying to think of who might have attacked Jacob. Sheriff Wright said he wasn't robbed. I thought maybe it was a robbery gone wrong, and the man fled before he could check Jacob's pockets."

Beth rolled out the dough and suggested, "He might have been beaten up as a warning to either himself or me, or maybe both of us. But I wouldn't put it past my father. Growing up, I heard teasing from the other children at school that my father was mean and hurt people. I thought it was all part of children teasing others. Now, I wonder if they were repeating what they heard their parents saying."

"You may be right," Rosy said as she lifted sausages out of the pan, placing them on a plate and sliding it in the oven to keep warm. "We'll close the diner after lunch and before we go see Jacob, let's stop in and speak to Sheriff Wright. I doubt there is anything he can do, but at least he will know about your suspicions. It might help him."

"I hope so," Beth said, trying not to cry. "Jacob is my friend, and it makes me sick to think my father could be responsible."

"Is he just a friend?"

Beth sighed. "I think I'm falling in love with him, but he doesn't see me that way. No, if I'm truthful, I have to say I'm already in love with Jacob Wheeler."

Rosy chuckled. "I think you're wrong. I think that's exactly how he sees you."

"Do you think so? I hope you're right. I pray he survives. I don't think I could bear it if he doesn't," Beth admitted.

"He's a strong young man, and we'll both pray. God will hear our prayers, and I think they'll be answered. Let's put those biscuits in the oven and then open the diner. I think we're ready to offer our customers a simple yet filling breakfast," Rosy said as she hurried to the front door, where several people were waiting for the diner to open.

Beth breathed a sigh of relief when Rosy declared it was time to close the diner after the lunch rush was over. She had tried to do her best, and though she mixed up orders a few times, everyone was gracious about it. They knew it was her first time stepping in to help Rosy, and that she was worried about Jacob. There were a couple, however, who wondered what in the world the mayor's daughter was doing working in a diner. Yet, the majority of folks in the diner today were just glad Rosy had reopened.

The men smiled and told Beth not to worry about the order, and the ladies patted her arm or hugged her on their way out. The kindness of the people of Palestine overwhelmed her. People she didn't know a month ago were kinder to her than her own father. Beth worried about her mother and hoped her father wasn't taking out his temper on her. She would try and see her this afternoon to make sure she was all right.

Rosy turned the open sign to closed and said, "We can finish cleaning later. Let's go see the sheriff and then head over to Doc's and see about Jacob. We can stop and speak to your mother before your father gets home, too."

Beth nodded and asked, "After we see the sheriff, I'd like to stop and speak to Mother quickly. Please come with me. I don't want to take the chance of running into Father. The maid can pack my things, and the stable boy can deliver them to your house. Can I keep them there until I get a room at the boarding house?"

"You can store them there as long as you wish," Rosy said, taking Beth's arm. "Let's go talk to Sheriff Wright."

The sheriff was behind his desk, rubbing Lep behind the ears, when Rosy and Beth stepped into the office. He stood and invited them to sit on the wooden chairs across from his desk.

Settling back behind his desk, the sheriff asked, "What can I do for you ladies?"

Beth looked at Rosy, and she nodded back to her. Then, Beth explained to the sheriff what concerned her about Jacob's beating.

Afterward, he leaned back in his chair and tapped his fingers on the edge of his desk. "Hearing what you said gives me another possibility to investigate. My first theory was a robbery gone wrong, and the attacker was scared off before he could rob Jacob. But that didn't seem right because he was severely beaten by more than one person. I tried to think of who wanted to beat him and possibly kill him. All I could think of was his connection to Sheriff Peel and you, Rosy," the sheriff explained.

"Me?" Rosy stammered. "Why me?"

Sheriff Wright shrugged. "I don't know. You're the only connection he has in town. At least I thought you were until I heard Miss Beth's story. An angry father is capable of doing a lot of things. Men have shot and killed their daughter's suitors. The problem is, I know the mayor didn't do this, so he must have hired someone, but who?"

Rosy shook her head, and Beth fought a losing battle with her tears, wiping her cheeks quickly as he continued.

The sheriff rubbed his chin with his hand. "Whether someone has a problem with Jacob because of his relationship with Beth or because he works for you, Rosy, I want both of you to be careful. I heard you moved out of the house, Miss Beth. Where are you staying?"

"Right now, with Rosy. I'll check at the boarding house for a room," Beth said.

Sheriff Wright thought for a moment. "I'd advise the two of you to stay together. If Miss Beth is working with you, Rosy, you two can walk to and from the diner together—you'd be safer that way. I know Rosy knows how to protect herself. If you're at the boarding house and someone tries to break in, there would be chaos."

"I know how to protect myself," Beth offered. "My grandfather believed women shouldn't have to depend on men for protection and taught me how to use a rifle and a handgun."

"Good," Sheriff Wright said. "You two look after each other, and I'll get to the bottom of this. With a little luck, we'll arrest the culprit soon."

Rosy and Beth thanked the sheriff and hurried to Beth's former home. Unfortunately, Dorothea wasn't there. Beth asked the maid to pack her trunks and have the stable boy drive them to Rosy's and leave them on the porch.

Stepping off the porch, Beth drew in a breath of relief. "I was worried my mother would be angry. But I'll see her soon, and at least I know I will have my things."

Rosy smiled. "Let's go see Jacob and the doc. I've been praying for good news."

"I have, too," Beth agreed, before the two ladies walked toward Reeves' office.

Beth stopped at the foot of the steps to Doc's porch and turned to her friend. "I'm afraid of what Doc has to say," Beth whispered as she reached out for Rosy's hand.

"We'll never know if we just stand here. I'll be at your side," Rosy said. "Come on."

Beth followed Rosy up the stairs and prayed when Rosy knocked and the door opened.

Mrs. Reeves smiled at the two women. "Please, come in. I'll get my husband. I'm sure you're anxious to hear about Jacob's condition."

They waited for the doctor in the comfortable parlor. Doc Reeves came down the hall and smiled at them.

"I think Jacob is going to make it. He's drifting in and out of consciousness and mumbling on occasion—it's difficult to make out what he's saying. I know he's said your name a few times, Miss Dubois, but I can't quite make out the other word. He's either saying 'can't' or 'don't.' Considering what happened to him, both words make sense."

"Could I see him, please?" Beth asked.

Doc nodded. "Yes, as long as you're quiet. You can speak to him softly but don't make any loud or disturbing sounds when you see him. His bruises are deepening, which is to be expected. His face looks worse than earlier, but that doesn't mean his injuries are more severe. It's just the body's reaction to the blows he endured."

"I promise I won't upset him," Beth said.

Doc nodded and allowed them into Jacob's room.

Beth's hands flew to her chest when she saw Jacob's body lying limp on the bed. The only movement was his chest slowly rising and falling with each breath. She was grateful that Doc warned her about Jacob's appearance. She sat in the chair next to his bed and fought back tears.

"Jacob," Beth whispered, "it's me, Beth. You're going to be all right. Doc said so and I'm praying for you."

Jacob's eyes fluttered for a moment, and she heard him whisper "Beth" barely audibly.

Beth leaned closer and whispered, "I'm here, Jacob."

Jacob's lips tried to move, and he said one word before drifting back to sleep: "Safe."

Beth looked at Rosy and she asked, "What do you suppose he means? Does he know he's safe here or since he said your name, is he telling you to be safe?"

Beth shook her head. "I wish I knew."

HOPING to learn what the town thought about Jacob's attack, Mayor Dubois planned on having lunch at the diner. He stopped dead in his tracks when he saw his daughter waiting tables inside the diner. *My daughter. How can she embarrass the family in such a crude way?* He would find a way to stop her just the way he would stop Jacob Wheeler.

The mayor strode back to his office, finding it difficult to hide the smile from his face. He needed to remain serious, giving others the impression he cared about the attack on Wheeler. He had hoped the man would have died, but perhaps the kid would heed the warning to stay away from Elizabeth anyway. If not, he could always take more action.

Walter Stanford, the mayor's clerk, looked up when Mayor Dubois entered the office. "I have the information on the city budget you asked for, sir. How is young Wheeler?"

"In a coma. Come into my office, I have some questions."

"Yes, sir," Walter answered, hurrying into the mayor's private office.

"I need this to stay in this office, so I'm asking you and not my lawyer. You did say you clerked for a lawyer, didn't you?" the mayor asked, not looking up from the papers on his desk.

"Yes, sir, but I didn't handle legal matters. Instead, I copied contracts and other paperwork and kept the books," Walter explained.

Mayor Dubois frowned and said, "I know it's the law that a man has control of his wife's monies, but do you know if he also has the right to control his adult children's finances?"

Walter shrugged. "I'm not sure, sir. I believe when a child becomes an adult, they legally make their own decisions."

"What if the child is unwell? Not physically, but in her head." Dubois put a finger to his temple. "Could a father stop her from spending money?"

"Possibly, sir."

Mayor Dubois nodded. "I need you to tell the banker I want to see him today. Go and hurry back."

Walter nodded and rushed from the office, returning a short fifteen minutes later.

"Mr. Woodworth will see you any time after lunch. His afternoon is open, but I'm not sure it will help you, sir," Walter explained.

"What are you talking about?"

"I assumed you were worried about your daughter, so I told Mr. Woodworth that you needed to inquire about helping her with her finances. He said he's not sure he can help you because there is some sort of legal constraint associated with Miss Elizabeth's account."

Anger flashed across the mayor's face, and Walter took a step back.

"Who told you to share any of my concerns with the banker? I needed to approach him with what I wanted to," he growled.

Walter took another step backward toward the door. "I'm sorry, sir. I was trying to help. You and I discuss all your business matters."

"Yes, between us. What's wrong with you? Elizabeth's finances are a family matter. Did you wake up stupid this morning?" the mayor fumed.

"Sorry, sir," Walter mumbled one more time before stepping through the doorway and closing the door behind him, wondering if the next insult from the mayor would cost him his job. No, the mayor couldn't fire him. He knew too much, and he'd share all he knew if pushed.

CHAPTER 7

"Well, Beth. You certainly saved my bacon today," Rosy said as she pulled down the shades over the windows and flipped over the open sign on the door. "Let's get these dishes washed up and then we'll drink a cup of coffee and go home."

Beth smiled. "Rosy, for the first time in a while I felt like I did something that was useful. I liked interacting with the people today, and if you think my work was satisfactory, I'd like to work for you."

"In the diner, Beth?" Rosy asked incredulously. She held up her hand. "I'm not saying that I couldn't use you or that your work wasn't acceptable, but you're a Dubois, the daughter of the mayor."

Beth threw down the wet cloth she was holding onto one of the tables. "Not you too, Rosy? You have the same look that my father had on his face when he came in here today and saw me with the apron around my waist, waiting on customers."

"Now wait a minute, Beth. All I was saying is that you might want to give this some thought."

"I have... and I'll ask you again. Would you like to take me on as an employee? Jacob's going to be unavailable for a couple of weeks and besides, you're my friend, Rosy... I want to help you. Is there anything wrong with that?"

With a big smile, Rosy reached and stroked Beth's face. "Why, dear, I would love for you to work here. And I'll pay you the same as I've been paying Jacob. How does that sound?"

"Wonderful," answered Beth as she picked up the cloth from the table and grabbed an armful of dishes to take to the kitchen. Rosy picked up the other items and followed her.

In no time, the ladies had the dishes and all the pots and pans they had used that day cleaned and put in their proper places to be used again the next morning.

Tired from being on her feet all day, Beth wiped her forehead and sighed. "If it suits you, Rosy, I would just as soon skip the coffee and head on over to Mrs. Downing's now. I didn't get a chance to check on a room today with everything going on."

"You know," said Rosy, "I was going to talk to you about that. What would you think of just staying with me for a couple of weeks? Remember what Sheriff Wright suggested? He said he thought we'd both be safer watching out for each other, especially until he can figure out who harmed Jacob and why."

"Rosy, I would like to stay with you under one condition."

"What's that, Beth?" asked Rosy.

"That you allow me to pay for room and board."

"All right. It's a deal. Your meals are on the house. You can eat at the diner. For the room..." She put her hand to her chin and tapped her lip with her index finger. "How about two dollars a week?"

"Rosy Baker, you've got yourself a deal." She smiled widely and held out her hand. Rosy shook it.

They blew out the last lamp by the door and closed up the diner for the night. As they turned to walk toward Rosy's house, two men stepped into their path, men neither woman had ever seen in Palestine, two of the same ones hired by Dubois to incapacitate Wheeler.

"Howdy, ladies. How about joining us for a drink across the street? We're new to town."

Out of fear, Beth stepped closer to Rosy, leaning into her. Rosy stepped in front of Beth. "No, thank you, gents. We've had a long day and are headed home."

"Home," the bigger of the two men said. "You mean the one two streets up, second on the left?"

Rosy's slight grin disappeared. She knew now these men were attempting to frighten her and possibly Beth.

Pulling a bottle from his pocket, the shorter man held it up and said, "How about a snort?" He reached to take hold of Rosy but quickly recoiled when he saw her derringer less than a foot from his forehead.

"Now, you fellers best find somebody else to pester, because, to tell you the truth, my friend and I have had a long day and we are not in the mood to be put upon. Now get!" ordered Rosy.

The men threw their hands in the air as if they were surrendering. Then, they backed away as one of them said, "All right, lady. We're leaving, but you haven't seen the last of us. The shorter man lunged forward in one last attempt to frighten the ladies. That proved to be almost a fatal mistake.

Rosy's derringer barked twice. The aggressor yelped as he bent over and clenched his side.

"She shot me," he groaned as he and his partner turned and trotted off.

When it was over, Beth stared over at Rosy. "Rosy, that was the bravest thing I've ever seen."

Rosy began to breathe hard. Then, she put her hands out as if she were dizzy or about to fall. Beth took her by the arm and asked if she was all right. Leaning against the back door of the diner, Rosy clutched her chest. "I'm shaking like a leaf in the wind."

Sheriff Wright turned the corner with pistol in hand. "Who's that standing on the stoop?" It was dark so all he could see were two silhouettes. He thumbed back the hammer on his Colt.

"Don't shoot, Sheriff!" Beth shouted. "It's Rosy Baker and Beth Dubois."

Woodrow quickly leathered his pistol and stepped toward them.

Striking a match, he held it up. "You two ladies hear a couple of gunshots?"

"Yes, Sheriff," answered Rosy. "They came from my derringer." She handed the small gun to him.

"Sure enough? Well, what made you fire this?" He held the gun in the air.

Beth spoke up. "Two goons were standing where you are right now. They tried to force us to have a drink with them."

Wright smiled and cleared his throat. "Well, I don't blame them fellers—two pretty ladies like yourselves."

"Thanks for the compliment, Sheriff," said Rosy, "but what those men were trying to do was scare us. One of them knew the address of my house."

"He did, did he?"

"Yes, and when his partner reached out to take hold of me, I peppered him good."

Woodrow struck another match and put it slightly above the ground. "From the blood in the dirt here, 'pears you got a couple of good licks in, Miss Rosy. I'll follow these signs. Maybe I can catch up to them. It'd be my guess they'll be headed to Doc Reeves. You ladies want me to escort you home first?"

"No, Sheriff, that won't be necessary. I still have a couple of shots left in this shooter." She took back her weapon from the sheriff.

Wright smiled and shook his head. "You're quite a lady, Miss Rosy. I only hope that I will find more women in Palestine like you, women who know how to take care of themselves." He touched his hat. "Good night to you, ladies."

They wasted no time getting home while the sheriff hurried back over to the jail to grab a lantern. Lighting it, he followed the blood trail the wounded man had made. Oddly, the signs did not lead to the sawbones, at least not immediately. They stopped just a few feet in front of Edward Dubois' house.

"Sheriff Wright. Can I help you with something?" came a voice from Dubois' dark porch. It was the mayor.

"Good evening, Mayor. I'm looking for a wounded man that accosted two of our women."

"Is that right? I certainly hope the ladies are all right," said Dubois with grave concern.

"Yes, sir. They are. Fact is, one of them shot the ill-behaved man. I tracked him to this spot." He held up the lantern. "There's a set of boot prints leading to your door. You haven't seen a couple of strangers come by here, have you, Mayor?"

"Well, no, Sheriff, I haven't. I just came out here to smoke my pipe and enjoy the fresh evening air." He stepped over to where the sheriff was standing and bent down to study the tracks. "Sure enough, looks like one of them came right to my door." He pointed with his pipe. "Wonder why he didn't knock?"

Wright thought it a bit odd that Dubois did not ask him for the ladies' names who were assaulted, but he wasn't about to volunteer the information. Already suspicious of Mayor Dubois, he bid him good night and started to walk on with the lantern held down to the ground.

"Sheriff, do keep me up-to-date on this matter," Edward said with his pipe between his teeth. "I am very concerned about the violence that seems to be taking root in Palestine. First, the Wheeler fellow, now two of our ladies. I will not tolerate this kind of behavior."

***

Early the next afternoon, Marshal Jubal Stone and Deputy Marshal Tanner Burns rode into Palestine behind Judd Roberts, the man who killed Monty Peel, and Dutch, the only man left of Roberts' gang.

The whole town was abuzz. Folks ran up and down the boardwalk yelling, some even screaming. They were visibly angry. The men who had killed their beloved sheriff were riding down Main Street, still breathing although they were in irons.

"I figured Marshal Stone would get him," yelled one man leaning against a post next to the mercantile. "You sorry dog, Judd Roberts. A rope is too good for you!" angrily hollered another man as he widened his stance, threatening to pull his gun. The crowd kept pace with the marshal and his deputy as they followed them down the street to the jail.

Jubal rode up beside Roberts with his Winchester resting on his knee. A part of him wanted to turn Judd and Dutch over to the mob, however, being a sworn officer of the law, he could do no such thing.

Roberts was not intimidated by the people, not at all. Through his battered, bruised, and swollen face, he said, "Well, Marshal. Looks like you've got your work cut out for you, protecting me and Dutch. Maybe you ought to shoot one of these townies. That'd make 'em scatter like a pack of rats." He laughed sadistically as he rested his hands on the saddle horn. It was more than Jubal Stone could stomach. Being in the same town with Roberts, the man who had killed his best friend, set him off. He was dog-mad.

Closer to the jail now, a buckboard sat unattended. Stone reached down and grabbed the stirrup Roberts' boot was in. Flipping him off the horse, he swung down and dragged him to the back of the wagon. "Now you'll get what you gave Monty, Judd."

He looked up to Tanner. "Throw me your rope." Burns didn't hesitate.

Jubal took the rope and tied Roberts' boots together then hitched him to the back of the wagon. Tanner drew his pistol and nervously held it on Dutch. He wasn't sure what the marshal had in mind, but he wasn't about to stop him, not this time.

Somebody ran and got Rosy. She came rushing down the boardwalk but suddenly stopped when she saw Roberts hogtied to the wagon. Jubal had asked the owner of the buckboard, Bruce Hawkins, to untie the team of horses and turn them loose when he told him.

Hawkins, not wanting to question the marshal's authority, did as he was told.

Rosy's fury burned. There on the ground, just a few feet from her, was a cold-blooded killer, the man who took her beloved Monty's life. All she could think about in that moment was the desire to end Judd Roberts' life.

Jubal barked, "Turn 'em loose, Hawkins." Of course, Jubal winked at Bruce when he said it.

Hawkins untied the horses and stepped back, staring incredulously at the marshal. He knew that Jubal Stone loved Monty Peel, but to send Roberts to his death behind a runaway wagon just seemed out of character for this lawman.

Jubal pulled his pistol and raised it in the air. "Go talk to the devil, Judd." He thumbed back the hammer and put his finger on the trigger.

Again, Roberts didn't seem fazed by the prospect of dying. "Marshal, you wouldn't deny me the rope, now would you?" he asked with a chilling laugh.

Jubal shook his head in disbelief. He'd not seen a man devoid of conscience like this since he tied up with Cable Lane several years ago, killing the murderer in a bare-knuckle fight. He began to lower his pistol when he heard the pop of a whip and a woman screaming.

Hawkins dove out of the way as Rosy laced the horses with the buggy whip and they took off with Judd Roberts dangling behind the wagon, black-snaked out of Palestine. The outlaw had gotten what he had given the beloved Sheriff Monty Peel.

Jubal ran toward his roan and swung up into the saddle. "Get Dutch into a cell, Tanner!" he yelled, then he wheeled Red and sunk his spurs into his belly. Within minutes, he caught up with the team of horses about two hundred yards out of town. Judd Roberts was just barely alive.

Roberts' reign of terror was over. His days of victimizing the innocent, robbing banks and trains, and killing lawmen had come to an abrupt end. Jubal had given him a painful beating just hours before coming to Palestine. Then, Rosy sent him up Main Street behind a runaway buckboard. Now, he would await a trial where a judge and jury would certainly send him to the gallows.

Sheriff Wright, aboard his gelding, met Jubal bringing Judd back to town in the buckboard. Red was tied behind. "Is he alive, Jubal?"

"Breathing, but that's about all."

"I'll let Doc Reeves know you're bringing Roberts over. I need to get this town settled down lickety-split."

U.S. MARSHAL JUBAL STONE TERRITORY

Woodrow wheeled his horse and galloped back into Palestine. As he rode toward the crowd, he waved the citizens out of the way. "Clear a path, folks. Got a man we need to get to the doc."

The people could now see Jubal driving the buckboard toward them, the one that dragged a killer out of town.

"Roberts won't need no doctor when we get finished with him, Sheriff," someone spoke up. "He'll need the undertaker."

Woodrow slowly climbed down from his chestnut and stared up at the man on the boardwalk. "Mr. Brooks, I believe it is? I'll have no more talk like that. We have law in this town, and I'm here to enforce it."

Sheriff Wright turned to the crowd and said, "Folks, I know Monty Peel was a good friend of yours, and you want nothing more than to carve Judd Roberts' liver out of him. But we've got to let the law take its course. He'll hang for what he's done just as sure as you're born. He'll hang."

Slowly, the people began to step back and clear a path for the buckboard Jubal was driving. He drove the horses to Doc's office and stopped. He and Sheriff Wright pulled Judd from the wagon and toted him through the door that Reeves held open.

"Put him in the second room down the hall," said the doc as he pulled off his glasses and pointed.

When Jubal and Sheriff Wright got Roberts into the room and on the bed, Reeves came in carrying his small black bag. "What in tarnation happened to this feller?" He put his stethoscope to Judd's chest and listened. Pulling the small ends from his ears, he shook his head and tugged at his ear, a habit the doctor was known for doing when he was agitated or concerned.

Neither Jubal nor Woodrow said anything.

"Judd Roberts, I suppose?" Reeves asked with raised eyebrows.

"Yes, sir," answered Jubal. "That's the polecat that done in Monty. Will he live, Doc?"

Reeves sighed deeply and swiped his hand over his eyes. "I think so, but," he turned to Sheriff Wright, "my wife and I can't look after both him and the Wheeler boy. He'll have to be taken to the jail."

"The Wheeler boy?" Stone queried.

"Yes. He's in the next room. He took a beating a few days ago that almost left him dead," answered the doc.

"Who did it?" asked Jubal with anger in his voice. He looked to Doc Reeves, then to the sheriff.

Wright shrugged his shoulders. "Ain't know for sure, but I've got me a pretty good idea who put the miscreants up to it. Let's go down to my office and do some jawing."

Jubal nodded but then looked to Reeves. "Can I look in on Jacob, Doc?"

Again, Reeves tugged on his ear. "Yes, but just for a minute or two. That boy's got a lot of healing to do."

Jubal stepped into the hallway while Wright assured Reeves he'd send a couple men to carry Judd Roberts over to the jail. As Stone stepped into Jacob's room, he removed his hat and eased over to the wounded man's side. He didn't plan on saying anything until Wheeler's eyelids began to flutter and then opened.

Whispering, Jubal said, "Well, hello, Jacob. It's good to see you, my friend."

Jacob smiled and blinked his eyes.

Jubal reached and squeezed his hand. "You get well soon. Is there anything I can get you?"

Wheeler slowly opened his mouth and said, "Beth and Rosy. Safe."

"You want me to make sure Beth and Rosy are safe? Is that what you're saying, Jacob?"

Jacob squeezed Jubal's hand and nodded. Then, he fell back to sleep.

Reeves was standing at the door when Jubal turned around. "You and Elizabeth Dubois are the only ones he's responded to, besides me and my wife. He must think a lot of you, Marshal."

"Obliged, Doc, for taking good care of him." Jubal pulled out a Gold Eagle. "There's more where that came from," he said as he handed it to him. "I've got to get on over to the jail and check on my other prisoner. See you directly, Doc."

U.S. MARSHAL JUBAL STONE TERRITORY

~

As Jubal walked into Wright's office, he saw Tanner sitting at the table, drinking coffee with the sheriff.

"Dutch give you any problem?"

"No, he didn't, Jubal. Almost wish he would have, though. Would have liked for him to get a dose of what Rosy gave Roberts."

Jubal smiled. "She's quite a woman, isn't she? I wasn't expecting that."

"You bet," quipped Wright. "Miss Rosy is a peach."

Tanner and Jubal exchanged stares, then they both looked toward the sheriff. "You ain't a little sweet on her, are you, Woodrow?"

Woodrow reached down to pet Lep. "Well, I'll just say me and Lep think a lot of her, don't we, boy?" he said as he held the hound's muzzle in his hands.

Jubal smiled and walked toward the coffee pot. "Man at the pot," said Tanner as he held his cup off the table.

Stone wagged his head. "Dang if you didn't get me again, Deputy. You're mighty fast on the draw with them words."

Jubal walked over with the pot in his hand and a cup. Pouring Tanner's cup full, he then filled his own. "Sheriff?"

"Nah." Woodrow waved a hand. "Got me something I need to get off my chest. Have a seat, Jubal, and you and Tanner lend me your ears."

Jubal sat the pot on the table and sat down in the chair. "All right, Woodrow. How can we help?"

Wright drummed his fingers on the table nervously. Then, his eyes darted to Tanner and Stone. "I believe Mayor Dubois hired them thugs to rough up Jacob and chase him off. Edward don't think Wheeler is good enough for his daughter. Miss Beth told me that herself, sitting right there where you're a-sittin'."

Jubal's anger burned as he continued to listen. "Sheriff, Jacob told me before we left town a few days back that he suspected Dubois had something to do with Monty's death."

"Well, by thunder," Wright pounded the desk with his fist, "why didn't he tell me that?"

"I don't know, but I'm starting to smell a rat."

"Yup, a big one," quipped Wright. "The plot thickens. Two nights ago, two men tried to assault Rosy and Beth at the back door of the diner. Rosy peppered one of them with her derringer." Woodrow smiled. "That Miss Baker—she's quite a woman."

Again, Jubal and Tanner stared at one another and smiled.

"Why would Dubois hire men to assault his daughter?" asked Tanner incredulously.

Before the sheriff could answer, Jubal said, "Because he didn't want Beth associating with Rosy." He peered at Sheriff Wright. "My guess is that she's been helping Rosy in the diner since Jacob's incident."

"By jingo, you're right. And that's not all." Woodrow scooted to the edge of his seat and put a finger to the table. "I followed the blood trail of that feller Rosy shot. It led a few feet from Dubois' house. Fact is, when I got there, Edward was out on his porch smoking his pipe. We exchanged words and he acted surprised about the tracks leading to his house."

"I figure to have a talk with Mayor Dubois. I won't bring any of this up, Woodrow. I'll just act as if I'm filling him in on the capture of Judd Roberts."

Woodrow pulled his watch from his vest pocket. "Follow your instincts, Marshal. You can probably catch him at his office a few doors up. He usually meets with the town council at ten o'clock on Thursdays."

"All right, but first I'm going to have a little talk with Rosy. Tanner, you want to come along and we'll get some supper? If you're all right with guarding the prisoners, Sheriff?"

"Yeah, you boys go ahead. I'll send some fellers over to Doc's to fetch Judd to the jail. Then, maybe the three of us can catch up later for a beer down at the saloon."

Jubal nodded then gestured to Tanner. "You ready?"

"I was born ready," quipped Burns. Then, he turned to the sheriff. "See you directly, Woodrow."

WHEN ROSY SAW Jubal enter the diner, she walked straight over to him, lowered her head, and said, "You here to arrest me, Jubal?"

Stone smiled warmly and put his arm around Rosy's shoulder. "Rosy, if you wouldn't have done what you did, somebody else probably would have. Doc Reeves says Roberts will live."

"Well, I can't say that that's good news," Rosy said with wrinkled face. "But I reckon I'm glad I didn't kill him. You fellers sit down there, and I'll bring you a plate of the special: beef roast and potatoes."

Jubal and Tanner plopped down and removed their hats. Just as they did, a young lady came bounding out of the kitchen carrying four platters across her arms. Stone pointed as he spoke to Rosy. "Is that the young Dubois girl?"

Rosy turned and smiled. "It sure is. She's quite a little worker, that one. Makes a mouthwatering apple pie to boot."

"Pretty little thing," said Tanner as he stared.

"Yeah… and taken," answered Rosy. "That's Jacob Wheeler's girl."

"Speaking of Jacob," said Jubal. "I just saw him lying in a bed over yonder at Doc's. Looks like somebody tried to kill him."

Rosy started to answer when the front door opened. Her hands balled into fists as she stared sternly. Jubal and Tanner followed her eyes to the door. "That's the vermin responsible for all of this. Mayor Dubois," said Rosy with squinted eyes.

"Congratulations, Marshal Stone, for bringing in Judd Roberts and one of his cronies," said the mayor as he stood over their table. "The Texas frontier is safer because of it. My compliments, sir, to you and your deputy." Dubois tipped his head.

"Obliged, Mayor. Would you care to join us? We were about to have the special."

"Why, yes, of course." He pulled out a chair and looked up at Rosy. "Miss Baker."

"*Mister Mayor*," Rosy said with utter disgust.

Jubal wasted no time with the evidence at hand. Even though he told Woodrow he wouldn't repeat what he told him, it seemed the right time to press Dubois.

"Mayor, what do you know about Jacob Wheeler's beating and the two ladies being harassed the other night right outside that door?" He pointed to the back door of the diner.

Dubois was the epitome of composure as he removed his derby, slowly hung it on the empty chair next to him, and pulled off his black leather gloves, finger by finger.

"Only what Sheriff Wright has told me, Marshal. However," he said, raising a finger, "I have posted a two hundred dollar reward for any information leading to the arrest of the assailants." He reached in his pocket and pulled out his pipe. "I expect someone to step forward any time now."

Jubal leaned forward and cracked his knuckles as he stared at Dubois. Then, his hands balled into fists as he laid his arms across the table. He knew by looking and listening to the mayor that he was guilty.

Just then, Beth walked by and cast an angry stare at her father. He reciprocated with a smirk.

Jubal's anger was at full chisel. He could see the evil in Dubois' eyes. Through gritted teeth, Jubal leaned forward. "Dubois, I've met a few men like you in my day. Come to a small town like Palestine so you could be the big hog at the trough."

"Now, see here, Marshal. I—"

"Hobble your lip… while you still have one. I ain't finished. It's a known fact that you hired those men to cripple Jacob Wheeler a few days ago and to frighten your daughter from having any association with Rosy Baker."

The mayor fumed as he sat and listened to Jubal's accusations. "I'll have your badge for this, Stone," he said as he pursed his lips then grinned acrimoniously.

"You'll get more than my badge if I can prove you had anything to do with Monty Peel's death. Roberts did a little talkin' on the trail." Jubal stretched the blanket a bit with his last statement but reading the mayor's eyes, he knew he had Dubois on the ropes, so he poured it on thick. "You're a snake in the grass, Dubois, and a scourge on the town of Palestine. Don't know why you left Louisiana, but you may want to consider going back. After these people find out what you did, they'll tar and feather you for sure."

Dubois stood to his feet and grabbed his hat. "We'll see what the sheriff has to say about this."

Jubal smiled. "Who do you think told me about you? Sheriff Wright is close to nailing your hide to the barn door, Dubois."

Stone looked across the room at the clock on the wall. "There's a train leaving Palestine in an hour. You might want to consider fetching tickets for you and your wife. Otherwise, you'll be facing charges and maybe even some prison time."

Dubois' demeanor suddenly changed. Arrogantly, he smirked. "You have no proof of anything you've accused me of. But this putrid, little, one-horse town of Palestine and this filthy hog-wallow called Rosy's Diner is beginning to grate on my nerves. Perhaps a relocation is in order."

A middle-aged couple sitting one table over heard the conversation. The man jumped up from his seat and, against the protests of his wife, confronted the mayor. "Mr. Dubois, let me be the first to say goodbye and good riddance. Since you've been our mayor, this town has changed for the worse." The fellow stood there waiting for Edward to engage him, but Dubois sensed his hostility and left.

As he stepped out onto the boardwalk, the mayor angrily reseated his derby atop his head, slapped his gloves to the palm of his hands, and started forward. Without looking where he was going, he collided with the sheriff.

"Excuse me, Mayor," said Wright as he grabbed hold of Dubois' shoulders with his hands to steady him.

Dubois stepped back, squinting his eyes at Wright. "Today I am resigning as mayor of Palestine. Please pass that on to the town council. The missus and I will be leaving immediately."

Woodrow was stunned by the news. He staggered into Rosy's Diner and Jubal waved for him to come over to their table.

"Dang if I didn't just have the most interesting talk with Mayor

Dubois." Throwing a thumb over his shoulder, he continued, "He resigned and said he was leaving town."

Tanner smiled, as did Jubal. Wright looked down suspiciously. "You fellers know something about this, do you?"

Rosy came to the table with three plates. "Where's Mayor Dubois?" she asked condescendingly.

"Funny thing," answered Jubal. "He just up and resigned. Figure he'll be on the next iron horse out of Palestine."

Rosy looked puzzled as she stood there holding three platefuls of food in her hands. Woodrow grabbed the white cloth laying next to the silverware and laid it across his lap. With a big smile, he looked up. "Is one of those for me, Miss Rosy?"

Jubal looked up at Rosy and she grinned. "It sure is, Woodrow," she said as she set it down in front of him.

CHAPTER 8

Beth heard the rumors about her father but couldn't believe he'd hire someone to frighten her. She and Rosy could have been hurt, or worse. She was still in disbelief until she saw her parents standing on the train platform, waiting for the morning train to arrive. Beth ran up to Dorothea who was doing her best not to cry.

"Oh, Elizabeth, I was so afraid I would never see you again," Dorothea cried as she hugged her daughter.

Beth glared at her father. "I hope you learned a lesson, Father. You tried to ruin my life and Jacob's. You've broken my mother's heart. If they could prove all you've done, you might have hanged. What a legacy for the Dubois family that would be."

Edward stood stoically, staring off into the distance. He looked at Beth but didn't smile or offer any words of endearment. He thrust out his hand and said, "Here is the key to the house. It's paid for. Your mother insisted that the least we could do is let you keep the house and furnishings. All the paperwork is on my desk."

"Thank you, Mother," Beth said, trying to ignore her father.

Edward grunted. "You might as well have it. I'm sure if we left town owning it, it would be burned to the ground or sold for a dollar.

Perhaps if you're going to live in it with that man from the diner, I should have had someone burn it."

Beth bit her lip hard, trying her best not to argue with her father. It broke her heart that he was responsible for Jacob's condition and worse.

When she heard the train, she hugged her mother again and said, "Write to me, please. I want to know where you are."

"I will, dear," Dorothea said before Beth turned and hurried away from her parents, feeling both sadness and relief.

Gripping the house key tightly in her hand until she felt it cutting into her palm, she found herself walking toward the house. Her house. She knew her father could be cruel, but she never considered that he was capable of criminal behavior in her worst nightmare until recently. She said a prayer for her mother's safety and strength to continue to live with her father because she knew her mother would never leave his side, regardless of what he did.

Beth stopped and stared up at the house. Taking a deep breath, she climbed the stairs and unlocked the door. The house felt empty. She'd been alone in the house before, but this was different. *Cold. Empty. Lonely.*

Hurrying to her father's office, she found the papers he said were on his desk. He had indeed signed the ownership of the house over to her. *Now, what will I do?* Well, fortunately she wouldn't have to impose on Rosy any longer as she could now live in this house.

Beth closed the office door behind her and walked to the stairs to see what her parents had left behind upstairs when she heard quiet sobbing coming from the kitchen.

Frowning, Beth walked into the kitchen to find Claire, the Dubois' maid, crying with her head cradled in her arms on the kitchen table.

"Claire?" Beth asked quietly. "What's wrong?"

Claire let out a small screech, jumped up from the chair, wiped her eyes, and stammered, "Oh, Miss Dubois. I'm so sorry. I shouldn't be here. Mayor Dubois told us to leave. I just needed some time to think. Please forgive me. I'll go now."

Beth waved her hands. "No, no, please sit back down. You have a cup of tea. Please drink it and I'll join you. I could use a cup of tea, too. Maybe you'll share why you're crying."

Claire sat back down and drew in a deep breath. "Your father came home last night and announced he and Missus Dubois were leaving for good. The cook, stable boy, and I were all dismissed. He said we would be paid what wages we had coming in the morning after breakfast."

Claire took a moment to breathe, sipped her tea, and continued, "He did exactly what he said. We were paid and your parents left with all their luggage. The stable boy drove them to the train station, came back, put the horse and carriage away, and left. Cook cleaned the dishes and kitchen and left, saying she could finally visit her sister in Denver. I was left here all alone."

"Why didn't you leave, too?" Beth asked.

"I intend to. I was just thinking of what to do and began to cry. I made a cup of tea and once I gained my composure, I was planning on leaving. Before your mother left, she called me into her room, handed me an envelope with an additional two months' wages, and apologized for her husband's sudden decision. I've been thinking of where to go and what to do," Claire explained.

"Can you go back to your family?" Beth asked.

Claire's face fell. "I am the eldest of thirteen children. My parents were pleased when I found this job. It gave me a source of income and a place to live. By now, my spot in the attic bedroom has been taken over, and if I went back, I would have to sleep in the barn loft."

"The barn loft?" Beth asked. "I can't imagine."

Claire smiled. "It isn't that bad. I've slept there before when one of my sisters was ill or just to find some peace and quiet to read. I'll miss the library here. I love all the books your father has. I suppose they're yours now. He said the house has been deeded to you."

"Yes, it has, and I intend to live here, but the thought of living in this big house alone is a bit daunting. Would you consider staying on? I promised to help Rosy in the diner, and I love working there. I could use some help taking care of this house and I'd like the company."

"Yes, Miss Dubois, I'd love to stay," Claire said, using the bottom of her white apron to wipe her eyes.

"Wonderful! But please call me Beth—Miss Dubois is too formal," Beth insisted.

"All right, Miss Beth," Claire said, smiling.

Beth nodded, wishing Claire would call her Beth and not Miss Beth, but she would change that in time. Right now, Beth was pleased to have a home and Claire as a housemate, even if she also worked as the maid.

Beth excused herself, telling Claire she needed to get to the diner and to make herself comfortable in the house. There was a lot of food, and Beth didn't expect Claire to work all day doing both her job and Cook's. They'd worry about meals later.

Rosy was surprised that Edward had deeded the house to Beth but understood that she no longer needed to stay with her since she had a place of her own now. Beth donned her apron and began working, telling Rosy that she'd work at the diner for as long as she was needed.

Rosy smiled.

~

TWO WEEKS HAD PASSED since her parents left Palestine. Beth pulled off her white apron and hung it on one of the hooks near the back door.

"Thanks for allowing me time each afternoon to visit Jacob," Beth said.

Rosy teased, "You're helping me. You don't need to thank me for some time off. Besides, that young man would die of a broken heart if you didn't visit him every day."

"I doubt that," Beth answered. "I think he cares from what he says and how he smiles at me. He's shared his plans for the future and asks my opinion, but I think what's foremost on his mind is leaving Doc's. They disagreed yesterday about when he could leave."

"Really?" Rosy asked. "Who won?"

"Doc for now. Jacob insists he should be able to go home, and if someone checks on him once or twice a day and brings him meals, he'd do well. Doc thinks another week in bed would be better."

"I suppose that someone would be you," Rosy said as she plunged her hands into the soapy dishwater.

"He didn't say, but he grinned at me. I wouldn't mind—once he's well," Beth shared.

Both women turned when they heard the small bell above the door chime.

"I'll take care of whoever it is," Beth said, grabbing her apron again.

Rosy grabbed a towel to dry her hands when she heard Beth exclaim, "Jacob Wheeler! What are you doing out of bed and here of all places?"

Rosy hurried out of the kitchen in time to hear Jacob answer.

"Doc agreed I was well enough to leave as long as I take and use this cane." Jacob laughed. "He said my sad face and pitiful voice were making his patients sicker than when they first walked in the door."

"Well, sit down and we'll bring you something to eat. Beth was going to visit you, but I'm happy to see you visiting us. You're going to listen to Doc and us and behave until you're well," Rosy insisted.

"Yes, ma'am." Jacob took a seat at a table near the kitchen.

Beth turned to follow Rosy into the kitchen when Jacob grabbed her hand. "Sit and eat with me, please?"

Beth smiled. "Seeing as how I was going to Doc's to see you, I suppose I could keep you company while you eat. Sit down… I'll just see if Rosy needs any help."

Beth returned with a plate of scrambled eggs, bacon, fried potatoes, and a cup of coffee. She took the chair across from Jacob and he said, "This isn't exactly the way I envisioned our first meal together. I planned to ask you for supper at the hotel."

Beth blushed. She had no idea why she was blushing except for the fact that Jacob was seldom outspoken like this. Supper together must be important to him.

Jacob didn't notice her shyness and instead dug into his breakfast as if he were starving. Between bites he managed to say, "Missus Reeves is a fair cook, but no one cooks like Rosy. Besides, her idea of food for strength is broth with a few vegetables. If I never have another bowl of broth again, it will be too soon."

Beth, hoping to add to Jacob's good mood, said, "My parents left town two weeks ago for good. My father deeded the house to me. They're never coming back. I don't think there was enough evidence to prove he hired those two men, but they can't be found anyway. Marshal Stone as well as the sheriff strongly suggested that Father leave and he did."

"I can't say I'm sorry they left, but why didn't you leave with them? I know I was attacked as a warning to stay away from you, but those men might still be close by. You'll be here alone now," Jacob said as he wiped his mouth on the white cloth napkin.

Beth smiled and answered, "I hoped I wouldn't be alone. I have that big house and someday I hope to fill it with children."

This time Jacob blushed and looked down at his empty plate.

Beth bit her lip to keep from smiling. She knew she had been forward by speaking of children, but she needed to give Jacob something to think about besides Rosy's meal.

When Jacob asked if Rosy had made any pies, Beth knew he was on his way to a complete recovery.

"She did. I'll get you a slice," Beth said as she picked up Jacob's plate.

"And more coffee, please?"

"Of course," Beth answered.

A few minutes later, Rosy brought out Jacob's slice of apple pie and sat down across from him.

"I put Beth to work for a bit so I could have a few minutes alone with you... Are you sure you should be here and not at Doc's home resting?" Rosy asked.

"I'm sure. I can rest at home. Doc suggested I use the cane and walk short distances at a time," Jacob explained.

Rosy stared at him for a moment and asked, "And meals, laundry, house cleaning? Can you do that?"

Jacob shook his head. "I hoped someone could bring me food, I can send my laundry to the laundress, and I never was one for over-cleaning."

Rosy laughed. "You need a caretaker."

Jacob shook his head. "I had one. Missus Reeves hovered over me."

"Well, you need one now. You need a wife. Ask Beth. I think she'd say yes," Rosy stated.

Jacob nearly choked on his pie. "Wife? I can't get married. I don't have any money. I don't even have a job. I'm hobbling around with a cane."

Rosy leaned closer and said, "You have a job here as soon as you're able and you have plans for the future. Beth has a home that's paid for. It's a lot more than many couples start off with. Think about it. A woman like Beth doesn't come into your life every day."

Jacob stared at Rosy with his mouth open and she smiled. As she made her way back to the kitchen, she thought she'd done more than plant a seed. She planted a tree that Jacob couldn't ignore.

CHAPTER 9

Four weeks had passed since Judd Roberts had been dragged through the streets of Palestine. Mayor Edward Dubois and his wife had left town. With his sudden resignation, a new mayor had been elected. Also, Jacob Wheeler had moved from the doctor's office and twenty-four hour care, back to where he was staying before his assault, Monty Peel's house.

With the use of a cane, Jacob was able to walk, but because of doctor's orders he was not to go any farther than his porch. Rosy and Beth were taking turns bringing him his meals and nursing him back to health.

Beth was still reeling a bit from her parent's sudden departure, but she was also excited about standing on her own two feet, something her father would not allow before.

It was two o'clock in the afternoon when Beth picked up the basket of food she had prepared for Jacob and stepped toward the door. "You sure you can handle things without me, Rosy? It seems like the lunch crowd is waning."

Rosy waved a hand. "Oh, sure, honey. Jacob's probably hungry for his lunch…" She smiled. "And I'm sure he's looking forward to seeing you. Have you heard anything from your mother, Beth?"

Beth frowned. "Not a word, Rosy. I'm worried sick over her. I know she had to go with Father, but I wish she could have stayed."

Rosy patted Beth on the shoulder. "I have a feeling your mother is stronger than you think, dear. She wouldn't want you to worry about her." Rosy pointed toward the door. "You better go check on Jacob."

With the basket in the bend of her arm and a mason jar full of sweet tea in one of her hands, she followed Rosy to the door and left the diner. She hoped Jacob would be showing more signs of improvement as he had during the last few visits she had made.

"Jacob Wheeler! Have you taken leave of your senses? What are you doing this far from home? I thought we agreed you'd wait for me to come to you."

"Oh, Beth," he said, breathing hard as he stopped and leaned on his cane. "That house of Monty's is getting smaller and smaller. Thought I would head over to the jail and say howdy to Sheriff Wright."

"You'll do no such thing, Jacob," Beth said with a finger pointing sternly at him. She grabbed his arm and put it on her shoulder. "Now, let's get you back home. Doc will have a fit if he sees you out here. Don't you remember him telling you not to go any farther than the porch?"

Jacob smiled but then a pain came over his body that made him almost buckle at the knees. Beth grabbed hold of his waist and said, "Lean on me, Jacob. I've got to get you back."

He didn't argue as he faintly replied, "Sorry I'm so much trouble to you, Beth."

She stared up at him warmly. "I'm glad I can be here for you."

When they got back to the front of Monty's house, she helped him into one of the chairs on the porch. Then, she set down the basket and tea and hurried into the house to bring back a blanket.

"Here, let's get this around you." She felt his head and didn't feel any fever, only sweat from the effort Jacob had put out from walking farther than he should have.

"How are you gettin' along, Beth, in that big house? I mean, I know you miss your ma and pa."

"I'm fine. Claire, the woman who was our maid, is living there with me. She didn't have a place to go, and I needed some help. However... I do miss them, my ma and pa, but it was time for me to cut the apron strings and find my own way."

Jacob smiled up at Beth. "I sure appreciate you and Rosy bringing me my meals and everything else the two of you have done for me. If I had the money, I'd pay you for all you've done."

Beth's face flushed red as she stepped back and stared angrily at Jacob. "Jacob Wheeler. Sometimes you make me so mad. When are you going to wake up and smell the coffee?"

Jacob's mouth flung open. "Well... Beth... I didn't mean to..."

Beth reached into the basket and pulled out a white cloth. Grabbing it by the corners, she shook it out and laid it over his lap "Just eat your lunch and don't leave this chair until I come back."

With a look of innocence, Jacob nodded. "I won't Beth, and... I'm sorry."

"I wish you would stop saying that," she said with great agitation in her voice. Then, in a softer tone, she continued, "I'm going inside to tidy up some things. Do you have everything you need?"

Jacob looked up at Beth's black, curly hair and her dark blue eyes and smiled. He wanted to tell her that she was all he needed and that he loved her, but he just couldn't muster the courage. "Yes, Beth. I do. Thanks."

In a few minutes, Beth returned to the porch with an armful of Jacob's dirty clothes. "I'll wash these up and get them back to you tomorrow."

"No, no, Beth. I can do that." Jacob stuttered, feeling mighty uncomfortable that she was holding his dirty laundry. "Please, just put them down." He made an effort to get out of his chair to take the clothes from her.

Beth dropped the clothes on the porch and gently pushed against his shoulder. "Okay, Jacob. I'll leave them. Just... calm down and don't get up."

He took a deep breath and for the next couple minutes they didn't say anything. Suddenly, Jacob spoke up. "That meal sure was good." He rubbed his belly and grinned.

"Rosy makes the best fried chicken in Texas."

Beth smiled and wiped a few crumbs from his jaw. "I'm glad you liked it, but it wasn't Rosy who cooked it."

"What?" Jacob replied as he pointed at the basket. "You mean, you fried up that chicken?"

"Why, Mr. Wheeler," Beth said with a grin as she packed up the basket to take back to Rosy's, "you act surprised that I can cook? You'll find that when I put my mind to something, I can usually get it done."

"Yes, ma'am. I certainly believe that. I certainly do." His eyebrows arched.

With the basket now in the bend of her arm, Beth started to leave. "Is there anything else I can do for you, Jacob?"

In his mind he thought quickly about how he'd really like to answer her question. *Yes, you can marry me, Miss Beth Dubois. That's what you can do for me.* But again, Wheeler was running a little low on courage. So, he thanked Beth for her help, said he had all he needed, and then said goodbye.

As Beth walked back toward Rosy's, she thought about her visit with Jacob. *Is that man ever going to come around to love? Why does he think I come by here every day to check on him, bring him food,* she looked down at the basket, *and clean up his house?* Then, she remembered Jacob saying that if he had the money, he would pay her for helping him. That thought put her on the prod. Arriving at the back door of the diner, she twisted the handle and stepped inside the kitchen. Still seething, she set the basket down on the counter without even noticing Rosy a few feet away.

"Well, how's Jacob doing today, Beth?" asked Rosy as she pushed her hair back with the back of her hand to keep it out of the dough she was kneading on the big, flat table.

Beth crossed her arms, frowned, and plopped down on one of the nearby stools. "Just fine. Jacob's *just fine,*" she answered irritably.

Rosy stopped what she was doing, wiped her hands on her apron, and walked over to Beth. "What happened, honey?" she asked in a soft tone. "Did Jacob say something that upset you?"

Beth pursed her lips and shook her head. "No, he was the perfect gentleman. In fact, he wished he had the money to pay me for helping him. Can you believe that?" Beth rose up from the stool, raised her hands in the air, and went on a rant as she walked briskly around the kitchen. "He wants to *pay me for helping him*," she growled.

With flour still on her hands, Rosy raised her arms. "Come here, honey. You need a hug."

"Yes, I do, because it doesn't look like I'm going to get one from him. Maybe some money, but nothing more. Oh, Rosy, I'm a mess. I ought to just leave Palestine."

Rosy stepped back, wiggled her nose, and shut one eye. "Maybe you need to take a little bit of a different tack with ol' Jacob." She shook her head. "I swear, he's as thickheaded as Monty was." Rosy held a finger to her lips then shook it in the air. "But you know, maybe, just maybe…"

"And just what are you cooking up, Miss Rosy Baker?" Beth smiled. "Don't just stand there. Tell me your plan, because I'm just about out of hope."

~

OVER THE NEXT FEW DAYS, Beth Dubois made herself scarce, around Jacob anyway, following her friend's advice. Rosy, instead of Beth, took him his meals and checked on him daily.

The first day Beth didn't come, Jacob didn't seem too concerned. But on the second day, he asked Rosy where she was.

"Well, she's had a lot on her mind lately. You know her ma and pa left Palestine and she's just trying to figure out if she wants to stay here or move somewhere else where she can get a teaching job."

"Move?" Jacob asked aghast. "Beth's going to leave Palestine?"

Rosy shrugged her shoulders and quickly turned the conversation away from Beth. "When do you think you'll be able to come back to the diner? I mean, I don't want to rush you or anything—just wondering."

Jacob seemed lost in his thoughts. His face puckered as if he'd just taken a bite out of a green persimmon. "I'm sorry, Rosy. What did you say?"

"When do you think you might be able to return to the diner to work?"

"Well, the doc tells me I'm making a lot of progress so maybe another week or two at the latest."

Rosy patted Jacob on the hand. "That's wonderful news. I sure have missed you."

"So, Beth is thinking about leaving Palestine?" Jacob asked with a look of consternation.

Again, Rosy acted coy. "Now, Jacob, I'm really not sure. That's something you'd have to talk to her about. I don't make a habit of meddling in other people's affairs. You know that."

Jacob tossed her a curious look. He knew Rosy thrived on gossip, but he did not argue with her. The thought of Beth departing Palestine had his nerves twisted into knots.

"Yes, ma'am."

Another day passed without Beth visiting Jacob. When Rosy showed up at his door with supper, he was noticeably annoyed.

"Is everything all right, Jacob?"

"Yes, ma'am." He pushed the door open so she could enter. "Miss Rosy, I'm obliged to you for bringing me supper, but I'm afraid I'm not up to talking this evening. Hope you understand."

"Sure, Jacob, sure. Now, I'll be back in the morning for those dishes." She pointed over her shoulder. "Have a good night."

As the door opened and closed, Jacob slumped down in his chair and stared at the food on the table. The last thing he wanted to do right now was eat. As he sat there chewing on his bottom lip, he thought, *I can't believe she would leave Palestine. Doesn't she know I love her?* He put his hand to his chin then slapped his forehead. *But how would she know I love her? I ain't never told her. You buckethead. What kind of man are you? You going to sit here and let the woman you love walk out of your life?* Then, another disturbing question flitted across his mind. *But what if she doesn't love me?*

The longer he sat there thinking, the more he stewed. *All this time I thought she liked me. Why did she come by every day if she didn't? Women. I just don't understand them, not at all.*

Jacob limped over to the table and sat down. Lifting the cloth that lay over the food, he picked up the fork and began pushing the roast beef around on the plate, never taking a bite. Then, suddenly, he slammed down the fork and said, *Well, by golly, if she won't come to me, I'll go to her.*

He rose from his seat with the aid of his cane and hurried over to where his clothes were hanging. Pulling down a clean shirt, he buttoned it, slicked back his hair, brushed his teeth, and headed out the door for the Dubois home. He aimed to see Beth Dubois and pronto, even if it meant walking four blocks to do so.

Jacob limped down the boardwalks and made it two blocks before stopping to catch his breath. All the walking caused him great pain, but what was burning in his gut right now surpassed any physical discomfort he was feeling.

When he arrived at the front door of Beth's house he took several breaths, checked the buttons on his shirt, and patted his hair to make sure it was in place. Then, he knocked at the door and waited with bated breath.

"Mr. Wheeler," said Claire as she pulled open the door. "Can I help you?" She stared at him curiously.

Jacob laced his hands together and held them up, almost as if in a praying posture. "Miss Claire, I was wondering if you could help me. I'm right sorry for showing up at your door at dusk but I need to speak with Miss Beth Dubois. Would you be so kind as to fetch her for me?"

"Why, certainly, Mr. Wheeler," answered Claire with a big smile. She opened the door and waved him in. "Please, come and sit in the parlor. I'll be right back."

Jacob nodded his appreciation and limped in, tapping his cane against the hardwood floor with each step he made. As he sat down on the plush, red sofa, he quickly rehearsed in his mind exactly what he'd say to Beth when he saw her.

Hello, Beth. It's been a few days since we've seen each other. I've really missed you. Can we talk?

Suddenly, he heard the sound of someone coming down the stairwell. He assumed it was Beth, so he rose to his feet and turned in that direction. But, to his disappointment, it was Claire.

"She'll be right down, Mr. Wheeler."

"Thank you, ma'am," he said nervously as he stared over her shoulder and up the stairs.

"My, my, our little town of Palestine has been abuzz lately, has it not?" asked Claire.

He was so engrossed in preparing to meet Beth that he didn't hear her question.

"Mr. Wheeler, did you hear me?"

"I'm sorry, Miss Claire. What was that?"

"I said, our town certainly has been abuzz with activity lately with that murderer, Judd Roberts being arrested, the mayor resigning, and..."

Again, there was the sound of someone walking down the steps. Jacob turned from Claire and peered toward the stairwell. That's when he saw Beth.

She hurried down the flight of stairs and grabbed Jacob by the arm. "Jacob, is everything all right?" Beth looked to Jacob, then to Claire, and then back to Jacob.

"Miss Claire, would you excuse us, please?"

"Why, certainly, Mr. Wheeler. Can I get either of you a cup of tea?"

They both shook their heads and thanked her for her kindness. Then, Jacob took Beth by the arm and limped over to the parlor. "Let's sit down."

Beth stared several times at Jacob as they moved toward the seating area. The look on his face had her worried.

As they sat down, Beth wasted no time. "What is it, Jacob?"

"Well," he said, stammering. "I..."

"Yes, Jacob?" she said inquisitively.

"I..."

Jacob got to his feet and rubbed the back of his neck. Then, he sat back down and stared at Beth. "I…"

With the intuition most women are known for having, Beth took a deep breath then leaned over and kissed Jacob on the cheek. "Are you trying to tell me that you love me, Jacob?"

Jacob closed his eyes and nodded. "Yes, Beth, I am. I do love you," he said as he moved to the edge of his seat and looked into her blue eyes. "And I don't understand why you are leaving Palestine."

"Leaving Palestine?" she asked incredulously.

"Yes. I know that you're hunting a teaching job and that there's no opening here, but…"

Beth smiled. "Have you been talking to Rosy?"

Jacob looked away, staring at the fireplace and the bed of hot coals still flickering red. He didn't want to betray Rosy but right now something was at stake that was more important than his relationship with his boss. Beth Dubois was about to walk out of his life, so he believed.

"Yes, I have, Beth. Now, look here," he said in a firm tone, a tone Beth had never heard him use before, "I thought you… liked me." He swallowed hard. "Maybe even loved me. Since the first time I ever saw you walk into Rosy's Diner I've loved you, Beth Dubois."

Beth scooted to the edge of her seat. Her heart was beating fast—maybe as fast as Jacob's. His words completely took away her breath.

Putting her hand to her chest, she said, "You have, Jacob?"

He grabbed her hand and pulled it to his lips. Kissing it, he answered, "I have, Beth." Then, he slowly kneeled to the floor, grimacing in pain. "Miss Beth Dubois, would you… would you be my wife?"

"Oh, Jacob, I will. I surely will." Beth looked over her shoulder and yelled for Claire.

"What is it, Miss Beth?" she asked as she ran into the parlor out of breath.

"Jacob asked me to be his wife and I said yes."

The two women hugged as Jacob tried to get up from the floor. He cleared his throat. "Excuse me, ladies, but do you think I could get some help getting on my feet?"

Embarrassed, Beth put her hand to her mouth and chuckled. "I'm sorry, Jacob. Of course, we can help you." She gestured to Claire and they hurried over and pulled him up from the floor.

"Congratulations, Mr. Wheeler. You sure are getting a wonderful young lady," said Claire with a smile.

Jacob nodded. "Yes, ma'am, Miss Claire. I couldn't agree with you more."

CHAPTER 10

The next morning, Beth and Jacob walked into the diner holding hands. "Rosy," said Jacob, "we've got something to tell you."

"Sorry I'm late, Rosy," Beth said excitedly. "But I wanted Jacob here when you heard the news."

"Well, by the look on both of your faces you better spill it before you bust." Rosy had a pretty good idea what their news was but didn't want to spoil it for the young couple.

Jacob started to speak when the first customer of the morning walked through the door of the diner. Beth looked to him then to Rosy. "Jacob asked me to marry him last night."

"Is that right? And just what was your answer, Beth?"

"I said yes."

Rosy hugged both of them and said, "We'll celebrate later. I better get some flapjacks on the griddle and bacon in the skillet. Jack looks hungry." The three of them looked over at the man who had just sat down at a table.

"I'll get him some coffee," said Beth.

"Let me do that, Beth," said Jacob. "It's time I started earning my keep."

They both strapped on a couple aprons and soon the diner began to fill up. For the next thirty minutes, Rosy, Beth, and Jacob stayed busy serving the customers.

When the restaurant was full to capacity, Jacob smiled and set down the coffee pot he was carrying. Moving to the middle of the room, he waited for Beth to come out of the kitchen. She walked by him, carrying four plates up and down her arms. After putting them down in front of the customers, she hurried back toward the kitchen. As she passed Jacob, she smiled warmly.

Jacob reached out and grabbed her arm. Twirling her around in a circle, he pulled her close to himself. Then, he gently pushed her away the length of his arm.

"Folks, can I have your attention?" he said loudly as he looked around the room. His eyes flashed to Beth then back toward the customers. Everyone in the room was surprised by Jacob's demeanor. Normally, he was quiet. Today he was making a loud announcement, so customers listened with great anticipation, whispering and pointing among themselves.

Beth was just as surprised as they were and waited for what he was going to say. Rosy pushed through the kitchen door and stopped.

Holding Beth's hand with his left hand, he leaned against his cane with his right and cleared his throat. "Folks, I asked this beautiful young lady here to marry me last night and she said yes."

The whole diner erupted in applause and congratulations. "When's the big day, Jacob?" asked someone across the room.

Jacob looked at Beth. "Well, we haven't decided that yet, but I don't see it being a long engagement."

His words caused Beth's heart to flutter with excitement and her face twisted into a big smile.

"How about a week from today? Would that be all right with you, Beth?"

As Beth stared at Jacob, she thought, *Now, isn't he something! A few hours ago, I couldn't get Jacob Wheeler to tell me he loved me. Now, here he is, telling the world that he loves me and wants me to become Mrs. Jacob Wheeler in a week!*

"A week from today will be perfect, Jacob. And I know exactly where I want to get married." She stared back at Rosy who was still standing in the doorway of the kitchen. "Would Rosy's Diner be available for a wedding?"

Rosy threw her arms in the air and ran toward Beth. "It sure will, dear." Then, Rosy looked to her customers. "And you're all invited."

Jacob pulled Beth into his arms and they embraced. Several people whistled while one said, "You sure you two don't want to move the wedding up?"

The man was elbowed by his wife, but that didn't stop him from posting a three-by-nine grin.

Suddenly, Beth pushed away from Jacob and a frantic look crossed her face.

"I've got a wedding to plan and seven days to do it. Oh, my goodness!" She threw her hands to her chest and held out her hand, counting off the things she needed to do. "I've got to get a dress."

"I have one you can use, Beth," said Rosy with tears streaming down her face. Her tears were a mixture of joy for the happy couple and sadness as she thought about how she and Monty were going to get married just one day before he was murdered.

Beth pointed to her fiancé. "Jacob, you'll need to speak to the parson." Before he could respond, Beth moved on to the next item on her mental list. Turning to Rosy, she said, "Rosy, you and I will need to discuss what we'll serve at the reception."

Jacob looked confused as his eyes followed Beth around the room. Rosy stepped over and put her arm around him. "It's okay, Jacob." She pointed to Beth. "That's what brides do."

A WEEK LATER, Beth, wearing Rosy's wedding dress that had been altered to her figure, was in a side room of the diner a few minutes before she was to walk out. There was a tap on the door.

"Come in," she said, "as long as you're not Jacob."

As the door opened, Beth looked up to see a woman dressed in a beautiful, lacy blue dress. It was her mother, Dorothea Dubois.

"Oh, Elizabeth Rose. I mean, Beth. You look… so beautiful. I am so happy for you."

"Mother! Oh, Mother. I'm so glad you came. Is… Father here?"

"No, darling, he didn't come. But I did." She held out her arms. Beth ran toward her and they embraced.

"I've got something I want to give you." Dorothea opened the palm of her hand. In it was a small pearl necklace.

Beth reached and took the dainty necklace from her and held it up. "Isn't this the necklace that Grandmother gave you on your wedding day, Mother?"

"It is, and I want you to have it."

"Oh, Mother!" Beth leaned in and gave Dorothea a kiss on the cheek. As she stepped back, she said, "Would you help me put it on?"

Rosy walked by the door to check on the bride. Beth looked up and smiled. Rosy winked and said, "It's time."

As Beth stepped into the hallway, Sheriff Wright met her and escorted her into the dining area. She had asked him to stand in for her father. Everyone applauded as she entered the room, including Jacob, who was standing next to the parson.

With a veil over her face, wearing Rosy's lacy dress and her grandmother's pearl necklace, Beth walked toward Jacob. As he watched her move toward him, never in his life had he seen such a beautiful woman as the one he was looking at.

That day, Jacob Wheeler and Beth Dubois became one in holy matrimony. They stayed in Palestine another three months before moving to Fort Worth where Jacob opened an upscale restaurant.

Ten months later, Beth birthed a son. They named him Monty, namesake of Monty Peel.

Made in the USA
Coppell, TX
12 September 2023